Praise for
MRS. SMITH'S SPY SCHOOL FOR GIRLS

"Middle-grade readers of Stuart Gibbs's *Spy School*
as well as fans of boarding school adventures such as
Shannon Hale's *Princess Academy* will appreciate this
comical and exhilarating escapade."
—*School Library Journal*

"A sassy, new spy series with a spunky heroine,
multitalented sidekicks, and tense, rapid-fire adventure."
—*Kirkus Reviews*

"A fast-moving, twist-filled addition to the kid spy genre,
which builds to a nail-biter of a conclusion."
—*Publishers Weekly*

"An action-filled romp . . . Abigail's entertaining
narration tempers suspense with levity, and readers will
have a blast accompanying her through sticky situations."
—*Booklist*

Praise for
POWER PLAY

"A celebration of friendship and girl power, this exciting spy story will keep readers on the edge of their seats."
—*School Library Journal*

"Fearless wannabe spy Abby's return in her latest fast-paced, intriguing, international escapade involving a complex computer game guarantees a rousing read."
—*Kirkus Reviews*

Power
Play

Also by Beth McMullen

MRS. SMITH'S SPY SCHOOL FOR GIRLS
DOUBLE CROSS

MRS. SMITH'S SPY SCHOOL FOR GIRLS

Power Play

Beth McMullen

ALADDIN

New York   London   Toronto   Sydney   New Delhi

This book is a work of fiction. Any references to historical events, real people, or real places are used fictitiously. Other names, characters, places, and events are products of the author's imagination, and any resemblance to actual events or places or persons, living or dead, is entirely coincidental.

⚱ ALADDIN

An imprint of Simon & Schuster Children's Publishing Division
1230 Avenue of the Americas, New York, New York 10020
First Aladdin paperback edition August 2019
Text copyright © 2018 by Beth McMullen
Cover illustrations copyright © 2018 by Vivienne To
Also available in an Aladdin hardcover edition.
All rights reserved, including the right of reproduction in whole or in part in any form.
ALADDIN and related logo are registered trademarks of Simon & Schuster, Inc.
For information about special discounts for bulk purchases, please contact Simon & Schuster Special Sales at 1-866-506-1949 or business@simonandschuster.com.
The Simon & Schuster Speakers Bureau can bring authors to your live event. For more information or to book an event contact the Simon & Schuster Speakers Bureau at 1-866-248-3049 or visit our website at www.simonspeakers.com.
Book designed by Laura Lyn DiSiena
The text of this book was set in Chaparral Pro.
Manufactured in the United States of America 0719 OFF
10 9 8 7 6 5 4 3 2 1
The Library of Congress has cataloged the hardcover edition as follows:
Names: McMullen, Beth, 1969– author.
Title: Power play / Beth McMullen.
Description: First Aladdin hardcover edition. | New York : Aladdin, 2018. |
Summary: When the creator of a new, popular reality game is kidnapped, Abigail Hunter and her friends go on their first official mission for the Center, and if they are lucky, they might just save the world.
Identifiers: LCCN 2018285775 |
ISBN 9781481490238 (hc) | ISBN 9781481490252 (eBook) |
Subjects: Spies—Juvenile fiction. | Kidnapping—Juvenile fiction. | JUVENILE FICTION / Social Themes / New Experience. | BISAC: JUVENILE FICTION / Girls & Women. | JUVENILE FICTION / Action & Adventure / General. | Adventure stories. | Kidnapping. | Schools. | Spy stories.
LC record available at https://lccn.loc.gov/2018285775
ISBN 9781481490245 (pbk)

For my father, Henry Van Ancken,
who always told good stories

Chapter 1

LEVEL UP OR GET BUSTED TRYING.

THERE IS NO WAY THE ALARM code for the McKinsey House dormitory door is wrong. I enter it again—7-A-4-3-P-X-*—but the light stays red and the door doesn't budge. I stomp my foot in aggravation, quietly of course, because breaking out of a locked Smith School dorm on a school night, or any other time, for that matter, is frowned upon.

If I enter the wrong code one more time, the alarms will blare so loudly they will wake the dead and certainly the McKinsey House dorm mother, who will find me here in the entryway, looking guilty. Toby swore by this code sequence. When he slipped it to me on a piece of paper in the dining hall earlier today, he even went so far as to give me a shaky thumbs-up and a slightly nauseous-looking smile. I smiled back, feeling it wasn't appropriate to mention he looked like he'd been run over by a bus. After all, Toby's one of my best friends and he did spend twenty-four seven for a week hacking the new alarm code generator before his dorm master noticed he wasn't showering or changing his clothes (gross) and Toby ended up doing a lot of dancing before the interim headmaster, who remained unconvinced of his innocence.

But now it seems the effort was for nothing. I have to go out the window anyway. The dorm is dark and smells like leftover pizza and this weird organic cleanser they use in the bathroom. That was one of the interim headmaster's changes. Plus she got rid of the gooey, creamy joy and happiness that was the dining hall's macaroni and cheese! Who does that? It was the only eatable thing they made. So what if it had zero nutritional value? Now they serve quinoa. We might as well eat cardboard. It has more taste.

I slip into Izumi's first-floor room. My room is on the fourth floor. To rappel out the fourth-floor window, a girl needs to tie together four sheets, increasing the risk of grave personal injury exponentially over, say, the first-floor window.

Izumi lies on her back, jaw slack, snoring like a freight train. I'm silent as the night until I trip over her rugby uniform, in a heap on the floor, and crash headlong into the bed.

"Abby!" she barks before her eyes even open. How does she know it's me? As if reading my mind, she says, "Of course it's you. Who else would be wandering around in the middle of the night? What happened to Toby's code?"

"Didn't work," I whisper.

Izumi pulls a pillow over her head. "The sheets are in the closet. Close the window when you go. I have a calc exam tomorrow. Good night. Go away."

I poke her in the thigh. "You're the best," I say.

"I know," she grumbles. I dig through her closet and find two sheets, still tied together from the last time I had to make a midnight window exit. I knot them around the leg of the desk and climb out the window, descending in the cold March darkness to the grass below. Now, the interim headmaster got rid of the mac and cheese, and that was bad. But she also fired Betty and Barney, the drooling, vicious, bloodthirsty nighttime guard dogs, and *that* was good. I'm no longer at risk of being torn to bits by animals lower down on the food chain than I am. I dash around the perimeter of McKinsey House, make a beeline across the quad, swing to the right of the slushy Cavanaugh Family Meditative Pond and Fountain, and pick the lock to one of the many doors into Main Hall.

Main Hall is the original Smith School for Children building. Everything used to happen in here. But this preppy paradise has grown. Now we have a science center and a technology building and a black box theater, and here's a tip: if you have money and want guaranteed admission for your kid, the school needs a new hockey rink. Apparently, the old one is looking "worn."

I creep down the corridor toward the headmaster's office, my heart doing a furious tap dance in my chest. I cannot get caught. Getting caught means I don't capture the Mogollon Monster, a giant smelly bigfoot with red eyes, who just happens to be a silver-level beast. More important, getting caught means I don't level up. And I need to level up because I'm losing. And I hate losing.

Just before I round the corner, I hear voices and freeze, plastering myself against the wall. It won't help. Sure, I'm wearing black leggings and a navy Smith School hoodie, but my sneakers are fluorescent orange and stand out against the big ugly portrait of Channing Smith, the founding father of our school, beneath which I huddle. No way I'm blending into that painting unless I'm a pheasant or a hunting dog.

I turn my smartphone facedown on my thigh so the green glow from the Monster Mayhem game doesn't give me away. And it looks like my luck might hold despite the code fiasco, because the bodies belonging to the voices don't turn the corner. They stop just short.

"Headmaster Smith *never* called us to her house in the middle of the night to *chat* about school matters." Oh, that has to be Ms. Dunne from the French department, a woman who could easily be mistaken for a parakeet. She's tiny and squawks a lot.

"I agree. And if the new headmaster is making the old headmaster look reasonable, well, that's saying something." This is Mr. Lord, chair of the English department. If Ms. Dunne is a parakeet, Mr. Lord is a giraffe. I want to giggle at the thought of them together, but I'm busy not breathing and blending into the big, ugly portrait. My phone vibrates. The Mogollon Monster is close.

"Do you suppose she ever sleeps?" Ms. Dunne asks conspiratorially.

"I don't think so," Mr. Lord whispers. "Vampire?"

"*Mon Dieu!* I certainly hope not."

"Well, vampire or not, something should be done. This is unreasonable. We have rights." It's the same tone he uses when we butcher Shakespeare in his class, like when

Toby burped in the middle of Lear's soliloquy. That got him tossed out with a warning about controlling one's bodily functions when in the presence of greatness. Did Mr. Lord mean himself or William Shakespeare? We couldn't be sure.

"Do we have rights?" Ms. Dunne asks cryptically.

"Why, of course we do," says Mr. Lord, although he doesn't sound convinced.

"Perhaps that's true, but let's take this up in the morning. It's late. Good night, Mr. Lord."

"Good night, Ms. Dunne."

I risk a peek around the corner. Mr. Lord and Ms. Dunne head in opposite directions toward their respective apartments on the upper level of Main Hall. I wait a full thirty seconds before doing a little happy dance. A good spy knows success is in the details, and this overheard conversation reliably puts the headmaster in her house across campus. And not in her office, where the Mogollon Monster hides. I can almost taste victory.

I continue quiet as a cat down the hallway. Monster Mayhem is all the rage. Earn points by capturing virtual mythical beasts. Catch enough and you level up. Level up and you can buy information about where to find more beasts *and* weapons to help capture them. And then you level up some more. But keep an eye on your health meter.

To stay in the green, you have to be actively capturing beasts. If it drops below red, you lose everything and bounce back to level one. It's very stressful. Chasing the *TADA!* that rings out after each capture is a full-time job.

At each level, the game gets harder. Bronze-level creatures are easy and plentiful, silver ones are more rare, trickier to catch, and dwell in complicated locations. Gold takes it up a notch, and don't even get me started on the platinum level. That's just pure madness. No one plays platinum. Rumor has it that there are bonus rounds at platinum where you have only a handful of *minutes* to capture a monster and if you screw up you're back to level one and a world of bronze. But if you win, total awesomeness. I think so, anyway.

Actually, no one knows what happens when you win a bonus round or win the game because it never happens, but either way, Monster Mayhem is perfect for spy training. This is *exactly* what I told the headmaster when she banned it from campus. No more *TADAs*.

Confused? A quick explanation: The Smith School for Children is just that, a fancy preparatory school nestled in the rolling Connecticut hills, churning out the best of tomorrow's leaders and all that nonsense. But hiding beneath all those Izods and docksiders, literally, is a small training facility for the Center, a government organization that uses kids to ferret out information no one else has any hope of acquiring. The theory is that kids are invisible (unless they're behaving badly, and then *everyone* has an opinion) and therefore make really good spies. But there are restrictions, and one is you can't be a proper spy until you are sixteen, which is torture because I'm ready *now*. And I'd make an amazing spy. Just last year, I uncovered the Center's existence as well as a traitor in our midst. I got really close to catching a notorious bad guy and managed to get the last headmaster sent on sabbatical for using poor judgment. *And* I discovered my mother was, like, head spy when I thought she was just a *mom*. What else does a girl need to do to prove her worth?

Of course, as you've probably figured out, the Monster Mayhem ban did not stop us from playing. It is simply a sick twist of fate that the Mogollon Monster virtually resides in the headmaster's office. Most of the monsters around campus are bronze-level werewolves. We rarely get something as exciting as the Mogollon, who's worth one hundred points and puts my health meter solidly back to green. It might even be enough to bump me to level six—still pathetic, but it's not our fault. We are trapped here, and that limits our opportunities to monster hunt beyond school. And while everyone freaked when the Mogollon appeared, no one has tried for him yet, not even Toby. Something about sneaking into the headmaster's office is so very unappealing. But if I can capture him, not only do I level up, I also get serious bragging rights.

After careful study, I determined Wednesday nights to be the only time during the week that the headmaster goes home at a reasonable hour. I think she reserves Wednesday nights for binge-watching 1980s movies on Netflix.

The massive door to the office suite is locked, but Smith recently got a 3-D printer, and Toby can't get enough of it. He made me a fine replica of the delicate filigreed key that the headmaster wears around her neck. He also made me a model of a kidney, which I did not ask for. This is just further evidence that Toby is weird. I slide the key into the massive oak door and wait for the sweet sound of the lock turning over. *Click.* I push the door open a few inches and slide in. It's pitch-black in the secretary's alcove. With my hands stretched in front of me, zombie-style, I take a tentative step and collide with a leather couch I could have sworn was against the far wall. I right myself and navigate around an end table and two bulky armchairs.

With trepidation, I open the door to the inner sanctum, the headmaster's sacred space and the location of the Mogollon Monster. I tap my screen and scan the room, trying to find his exact location. My bronze cage is ready. It looks like he's behind the desk. I take one small step and another. I stub my toe on a table and catch the toppled lamp a mere millisecond before it crashes to the wood floor. Sweat gathers on my forehead. This seemed much easier in theory.

But I'm committed! They might not let me be a spy, but I can capture Monster Mayhem beasts like nobody's business. I scan again. The Mogollon Monster is definitely behind the desk. And he knows I'm coming for him. He bares his teeth and growls. Gobs of saliva drip from his mouth. His eyes flash red. I know he's not real, but he scares me a little anyway.

I'm almost to the door when a cold hand covers my mouth from behind. Naturally, I scream and drop the phone, frantically trying to bite the hand, but it's clamped on too hard. What do I know about defending myself against an attacker coming from behind? Oh, right. Nothing. I kick my feet and flail my arms. A ceramic container flies off the desk and smashes on the floor. Paper clips scatter everywhere. I scream again and continue to struggle uselessly.

"I think you're overreacting," my attacker says calmly.

Wait. What? The grip on my mouth loosens and I gasp for air, turning slowly to face the interim headmaster But she just met with Ms. Dunne and Mr. Lord at her house *all* the way on the other side of campus. There is no way she could have gotten here this fast. The nervous adrenaline drains away, and my shoulders sag. Maybe she *is* a vampire? It doesn't matter. I've failed. The Mogollon Monster is gone.

"Oh, come on," the headmaster says. "It's not as bad as all that. It's just one beast."

"An important beast," I mutter, leaning into her desk, defeated. "Can I go?"

"No." She paces in front of the large windows. She never used to pace. She used to chew her cuticles. She's changed. "You've got to stop breaking the rules. It makes me look bad."

"I'd behave if you let me be a spy," I say.

"You're too young," she snaps. "Be patient."

I'm really bad at being patient. "But . . ."

"But nothing," she says, her eyes narrowing. The

interim headmaster is not inherently scary, but when she looks at you a certain way, your mouth goes dry regardless.

"Okay," I say quietly. I await the verdict on my punishment for sneaking out of my dorm, breaking into Main Hall, and chasing monsters.

But the headmaster's eyes soften. "Go to bed," she says with a sigh. "It's the middle of the night. And please use the dormitory door. The next time you climb out a window after curfew to play this ridiculous game, or for any other reason, I'll have you scrubbing algae off the bottom of the pond with a toothbrush next to Tucker Harrington."

Boy, that's low. Tucker Harrington is a big dumb bully whose popularity I just don't understand. She lessens the blow by planting a kiss on my head. "I love you, sweetie," she says. "Even though sometimes you drive me crazy."

And I say, "Good night, Mom."

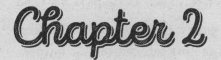

Chapter 2

IT'S REALLY BORING
UNTIL IT'S NOT.

WE HUDDLE AT OUR USUAL breakfast table in the vast Smith School dining hall—me, Izumi, Charlotte, and Quinn (my best friends, minus Quinn). An assortment of food with no discernible nutritional value is laid out before us. Lucky Charms, Pop-Tarts, bread layered one inch thick with butter and marshmallow fluff. The interim headmaster has taken control of dinner and lunch. Breakfast is next on the hit list. Soon all these wonderful empty calories will be history. It's enough to make a girl cry all over her glazed chocolate donut.

On the walls hang posters encouraging us to get ready for the annual Spring Fling Formal. Even the name is fun! Like a barrel of monkeys! Yes. Perhaps if the monkeys are rabid. Spring Fling, aka Fake Prom, is meant to keep Smith seniors from feeling left out of this barbaric American rite of passage. Except in our case, the torture is not reserved just for the lucky seniors. The whole school is invited. Even us Middles. (A side note: in the normal world, Lower Middles would be seventh graders, Middles eighth graders, and Upper Middles ninth graders. The middle of what? We have no idea.)

Now, even though we're not invisible like the Lower Middles, we are certainly less than socially acceptable. At Fake Prom, Lower Middles are expected not to come, and Middles, if they are brave enough to show up, must remain in the shadows. What would happen if a Middle dared bust a move on the dance floor? Armageddon, that's what. I refused to go last year, and I plan on refusing to go this year. Not that the boys are exactly beating down the door to ask me, but you understand what I mean.

"Nice going last night," Quinn says with a smirk, bits of frosted strawberry Pop-Tart spraying from his lips. Everyone knows about my failure. The spread of information on social media has got nothing on boarding school. They probably knew I'd screwed up before I was actually done doing it. It explains the side-eyes and snickers served up with my hot chocolate.

"I have no idea what you're talking about," I say curtly.

"Did you really think you stood a chance against Jennifer Hunter?" he asks.

"Shut up," Charlotte snaps. This works. Quinn is completely and totally obsessed with Charlotte, while she finds him boring. Her exact description is "He's a cookie-cutter, preppy, polo-wearing brat from Greenwich, Connecticut, with no edges."

But he will not give up. He's asked her to Spring Fling fifteen times. Definition of an idiot: someone who does the same thing over and over and expects a different result.

"Where's Toby?" I ask, changing the subject. Usually, Toby's the first one here, cup of coffee in one hand, tablet in the other, inevitably in the middle of some violent, blood-soaked, totally age-inappropriate video game where he's meant to destroy everything and save the world. We're not supposed to have coffee (only for faculty and staff), and we're not supposed to have electronics (nothing more advanced than a pencil and paper from breakfast until the end of classes). But nobody has ever accused Toby of being a rule follower.

"Don't know," says Quinn. He stuffs the second half of the Pop-Tart into his mouth. There are a handful of things that make boarding school bearable, and the Pop-Tarts hover near the top of the list. There might be a revolution if they are removed from the dining hall. See how the interim headmaster deals with a horde of sugar-deprived teenagers showing up at her door. It will make all those secret missions she went on that she never bothered to *tell* me about seem like a vacation.

"He's probably with his dad," Izumi offers. "Drexel is doing school meeting lecture this morning." There's a collective groan at the table. Every morning, we have a mandatory school meeting in the cavernous Main Hall auditorium. We sit in assigned seats, and several seniors loom large in the balcony overhead, charged with taking attendance. If your seat is empty, you get demerits. Now, the seniors don't care if you pay, bribe, or threaten someone to sit in your seat as long as a warm body is present and accounted for. Last year, a student tried a mannequin dressed in the Smith uniform, but one of the arms fell off, and that was a dead giveaway.

School meeting consists of announcements—Boys' lacrosse tryouts! Join the creative writing club! Save the endangered African rhino!—followed by a short twenty-minute lecture on any number of character-building top-ics. We are supposed to leave school meeting inspired for a day of excellence, but mostly we nap. Today, the esteemed Drexel Caine will be our speaker. In addition to being Toby's dad, Drexel is an inventor, scientist, collector of weird things, and, most important, owner of DrexCon. DrexCon is responsible for Monster Mayhem, the augmented reality game that has devoured the world and came very close to getting me in heaps of trouble last night. Drexel is also a member of the Smith School board of trustees, but rumor has it no one has bothered to tell him.

I'm sure Drexel is a perfectly nice man, but we don't like him because he's a parent, and parents are the ones who parked us here. We refer to all parents by their first names in an effort to restore the balance of power. This is an abject failure, but we stick with it on principle. Back in September, Drexel missed Toby's birthday *and* Parents' Weekend, without even so much as a phone call. He was giving a speech in Geneva, where they appear not to have phones. Three weeks later, he sent Toby a fancy leather jacket from a store in London. Toby wears the jacket whenever we're out of school uniform but claims he does so ironically. The only time I've seen Toby and Drexel together, Drexel was stuck somewhere between bored and anxious, and Toby just looked sad. I guess being the only son of a genius isn't easy. Neither is being the daughter of a superspy interim school headmaster.

The bell rings, indicating we have exactly four minutes to get to school meeting. A surge of students in blue blazers, khaki pants, and pleated skirts push out the wide doors of the dining hall and move like a wave down the long broad corridor toward Main Hall.

At some point, Toby joins the parade. "Your code didn't work last night," I mutter under my breath.

He shrugs me off. "You probably entered it wrong."

"Did not."

"Human error accounts for most problems with technology."

"Not mine."

"Yes, yours."

"You messed it up."

"Did not."

"Whatever," I say. But we're friends, I swear.

"Is Drexel speaking today?" Izumi asks.

"Yes," Toby says, rolling his eyes. "Are you guys prepared to be bored to death?"

"Why should today be different from any other day?"

asks Charlotte. It's not unusual to have parents of students give school meeting minilectures. We've had scores of famous authors, medical pioneers, business titans, and politicians. Drexel Caine, for example, is world-famous, but that doesn't mean we care.

"Is he going to demo any new DrexCon games?" asks Quinn anxiously.

Toby looks at him as if he's sprouted a new head. "Games? At Smith? Jennifer will take him down from fifty yards with a blow dart if he even *mentions* DrexCon." Jennifer banned Monster Mayhem and all other augmented reality games from campus after a Lower Middle fell in the pond chasing a werewolf. She said she would not sit by while we turned into mindless zombies. You now play at your own risk, as I demonstrated last night. "No. He's here to talk about resilience."

"Well, that's exciting," I say. Yesterday's school meeting was about dignity. Apparently, that's something to strive for. The wave of students slows as we squeeze into the auditorium. Once inside, we spread out in search of our seats. None of our assigned seats are together. This is not an accident.

By the time Drexel steps behind the podium, I've had

a series of five or six quick naps and missed every single announcement. I'm sure there was nothing important. Besides, I'm not very good at saving rhinos, and I'd make a terrible boys' lacrosse player.

Drexel is a tall, thin man with close-cropped hair. His wrinkled suit hangs from his narrow shoulders. Perched on his head is a pair of thick plastic sunglasses that he can't stop fiddling with. He leans down and taps the microphone a few times. The thumps echo through the large auditorium.

"Guess it's on," he says, left hand floating to the sunglasses. "Well, hi, guys. Glad to be here at . . ." The pause is long enough that it's clear Drexel Caine has temporarily forgotten where he is. I cast a sideways glance at Toby, six seats down. He studies his shoes.

"Smith!" Drexel shouts suddenly, looking proud for remembering before things got really awkward. "Yes, indeed. The Smith School for Kids. Or children. Or whatever. I'm supposed to talk about resilience. I'm *not* supposed to talk about Monster Mayhem 2.0, releasing next month." A spontaneous roar goes up from the student body. "But let me tell you it's awesome. New beasts, new levels, new challenges. You'll be *hooked*." He looks out at us with a sly grin. "But I promised the headmaster. Of course, if you *really* want to know how cool the update is, you can ask Toby. He's been playing it for a while." Drexel squints out over the crowd, looking for Toby. Toby slides so low in his seat he's in danger of landing on the floor. I give him a smile that I hope conveys my sympathy. Parents can be difficult, embarrassing, and generally awful exactly at the moment you don't want them to be. Trust me, I know. After all, my mother is the headmaster.

Up onstage, Drexel wrestles the microphone from its holster on the podium, simultaneously wrapping the cord around his legs and almost falling on his face. The student body gives a collective gasp, but Drexel saves himself at the last second.

"Well, this is so exciting," he says, stepping out of the tangle at his feet. "Being here with you guys. And we're talking about . . ." There goes that temporary separation from reality again.

"Resilience!" someone shouts.

"Right!" Drexel says, his face brightening. "You have got to be willing to screw things up really badly over and over again if you want to succeed. That's resilience. Get back on the horse!" He paces the stage, dragging the microphone cable behind him like a reluctant dog. "Or the bike! Or whatever metaphor works for you. Just don't give up. Okay? Got that?" This has the beginnings of a classic Drexel-style rant. There's a really good chance he blows through his allotted twenty minutes and we end up trending on YouTube.

He's at the far end of the stage when he holds a hand up to shield his eyes, peering into the back of the dark auditorium. His face twists with acute concern. "Well, that's strange," he says quietly. "I haven't seen him in ages. How did he get in here?"

What happens next is a loud explosion, a scream, and an auditorium billowing with smoke.

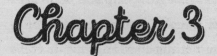

Chapter 3

NOTHING HAPPENED.
NO, REALLY.

WE'RE PLUNGED INTO DARKNESS. Fire alarms wail, red exit lights flash, and a cascade of water rains down on us from the sprinklers overhead. As students surge toward the rear exits, I'm propelled out of my seat and swept into the aisle. Ms. Dunne's shrieking parakeet voice cuts through the chaos. "Children, be calm! Single file! Slowly!" The students choose none of the above and press toward the doors. There are 627 students at Smith, and this is the first time we've ever succeeded in all doing the same thing at the same time. If not for the questionable nature of the events (the building might actually be on fire), I'd say we were to be congratulated.

On the slick, wet floor, kids begin to slip and fall. That's when I push out of the rush like a swimmer escaping a riptide and plaster myself against the auditorium wall. If it's a choice between death by smoke inhalation or trampling, I choose, well, neither actually, but the crowd is way too scary. Seconds later, Izumi is pressed to the wall beside me, panting.

"What happened?" she gasps.

"I think we're on fire," I say.

"Not good."

"No."

"Come on," she says, taking my hand. "Stay with me." Izumi is about as wide as she is tall and is very happy to use her body as a battering ram. About halfway up the aisle, I spy Charlotte and grab on to her, making a chain. Ms. Dunne bellows for calm. I can see out the big auditorium doors to the hall beyond. A dozen teachers fly in our direction, led by Jennifer. She screeches to a stop when she arrives at the mass of students and immediately begins barking orders at her teachers. "You, begin head count! You, triage! You, get these children outside!" Her eyes scan the crowd, panicky, until they find mine. When she sees me, she visibly relaxes and returns to her role as benign dictator. Charlotte, Izumi, and I are carried outside of Main Hall on the tide just as a brigade of fire trucks come screaming into the circular driveway. We leap out of the way as a dozen firefighters rush the building. It's all very dramatic. Even Charlotte is speechless.

Ten minutes later, those same firefighters trudge back out. Yes, there was a lot of smoke, but there was no fire. The smoke came from a machine. This was all some elaborate prank. While on one level I'm deeply impressed, I also would not want to be the kid when he or she gets caught, and getting caught is inevitable. Come on! There's a spy school in the basement! Pranks of this nature are very high-risk.

Outside we're organized into little wet flotillas and counted and sorted. Everyone is here except for Nathan Winters, who's asleep in his dorm room on the other side of campus. This would not be the first time Nathan slept through mandatory breakfast and school meeting. He has so many demerits he's actually on tap to clean bathrooms until he's forty-five.

Finally, we're dismissed. In fifteen minutes, we'd better be dry and in class. As the group dissolves, everyone sagging after the adrenaline rush of possible danger, Jennifer strides up to us.

I put up my hands defensively. "It was *not* us. We were in school meeting. You can check the attendance."

She waves me off. "I know. I know. Toby, have you seen your father?"

"Who?" asks Toby, raising an eyebrow.

Jennifer sighs, exasperated. "I did not ask if you *like* your father, Toby. I just want to know if you've seen him since the . . . mishap."

"He doesn't like crowds," Toby says. "Probably he jumped in his limo and went home."

"Did he say good-bye to you?" Jennifer asks.

"Why would he do that?"

Jennifer exhales sharply. She never used to do that either. I think being headmaster is more trouble than she expected. I bet some nights she wishes Mrs. Smith would hurry up and get rehabilitated or whatever and come back.

"You'd better hurry or you'll be late to class," she says finally, and we squish our way back to our respective dorms.

The rest of the day is downright boring by comparison. The teachers all seem twitchy, as if they expect smoke and alarms and chaos around every corner. I'm late to Chinese History 2 with Mr. Chin, and he gives me dirty looks through the entire class. The lunch choices all have kale in them. It's raining, and I arrive at the squash courts for practice covered in mud. Squash is a terrible game where the players are locked in a four-walled court and expected to smack a little rubber ball around until someone wins. Unfortunately, sports are required at Smith. When I suggested spy training could count as a sport, Jennifer kicked me out of her office.

By the time we get to dinner, everyone has pretty much had it with the day. At least it's Wednesday, which means no formal dinner with assigned tables. We eat cafeteria-style and can sit with our friends. Charlotte, Izumi, and I join a table with Toby and Quinn and a few other boys, the names of whom I cannot be bothered to remember. Quinn shoves one of the nameless boys out of his chair and onto the floor so Charlotte can sit next to him. She doesn't. He looks crestfallen. When will he learn?

Toby picks at his quinoa. Usually, he eats everything on his own tray and then starts in on mine. But tonight he practices a ten-mile stare. I nudge him with my shoulder.

"What's wrong with you?" I ask. "You haven't blinked in, like, two minutes. It's creepy."

His eyes dart around the room, unsettled, searching. He won't meet my gaze. "What? Sorry. Just thinking."

"About what?"

"Nothing," he says, too quickly.

A prickly sensation runs up my spine. The tiny hairs on the back of my neck stand up. Something is not right. "How come I don't believe you?"

"Just leave it, Abby, okay?" he snaps, pushing back from the table. He barges out of the dining hall without another word. We all stare after him.

"What's with him?" asks Charlotte.

"I have no idea," I say.

"He's been weird all day," says Quinn. "Since the thing this morning."

"Do you think he's upset because his dad left without saying good-bye?" Izumi asks. One thing I know for sure about Toby is he has an aversion to drama. He'd rather swim a length of the Cavanaugh Family Meditative Pond and Fountain in his underwear than be compared to someone like Charlotte, for whom drama is a second language. Even if he were upset, storming away from the dinner table is not his style.

And I tell you this is why I'd make a great spy! I have a sense for when things are not as they should be. Of course, you might remind me at this point that I lived with Jennifer for twelve years before figuring out she was a spy, but that was *training*. I was getting ready for the big game.

Now I just have to convince them to let me play. I throw my napkin on my plate. "I'll be right back."

I catch a glimpse of Toby's neon orange hoodie as he rounds the corner, headed back to his dorm. Picking up the pace, I catch him just as he gets to the stairs. I skid to a stop and grab his arm.

"Wait!" I yell.

He jumps in surprise. "Abby!"

"Sorry," I say. "Are you okay?"

"I'm fine." But his face is tight. If he's trying to convince me of his fineness, he's just failed spectacularly.

"You're so not."

"What part of *leave me alone* didn't you understand?"

"I'm going to choose not to respond to that." I sniff.

"Whatever." He tries for the stairs, but I still have his arm and I'm not letting go.

"Listen," I say. "I know boys don't talk about things—"

"Quinn does," Toby interrupts. "Quinn never stops talking. And what he talks about is Charlotte."

Yes, I can see how that would get old, but Toby doesn't care about Quinn's chattiness. He actually likes it because it means he never has to be the center of attention. But right now he's trying to redirect my attention. It won't work. "That's nice, but I don't care about Quinn at the moment."

"Can you just go?" he pleads.

"No," I say. "Spill it."

He really doesn't want to. His whole body tells me to go away. "We're friends, Toby," I remind him. Toby is not Charlotte or Izumi, but I would still do anything for him. And I'm pretty sure he feels the same about me. Maybe? His shoulders sag as he digs in his pocket for his phone.

"Look at this," he says, handing it to me. "And try not to freak out."

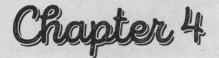

Chapter 4

SURE. I CAN KEEP A SECRET. FOR EXACTLY ONE HOUR.

ON THE SCREEN IS MONSTER MAYHEM. Not the old version, the one I have, but a new one that's so crisp and bright, I have to blink a few times. Toby's avatar, a cartoony superhero version of himself, fills the screen. Toby is the Smith School's undisputed Monster master. He's a silverlevel seventy-eight, and he'd definitely be on the Monster leaderboard that DrexCon keeps on their website if he weren't physically trapped here at Smith, like the rest of us. Currently, Iceman is in first place. Rumor has it Iceman is a dastardly underworld dark web villain who is also good at Monster Mayhem.

Six empty platinum cages hang above the avatar's head.

Platinum level. *Uh-oh*. The background is a blurred-out map.

"Is this 2.0?" I ask, suddenly breathless.

Toby pinches the bridge of his nose. "Yes. Drexel insisted I test it myself, like it was some sort of honor or reward."

"So *why* are you upset?" Any kid in this school would kill to have access to Monster Mayhem 2.0. The entire world is counting down the days until its release. I'm about to launch an interrogation into why he's been hoarding the new version, but something in his face stops me. He taps the bottom of the screen and a message bubble appears. The words are written in all caps, like a big ugly shout in the face.

WELCOME TO THE GAME
OF YOUR LIFE!

**MENACE SAYS IF YOU CAPTURE
FIVE EPIC PLATINUM-LEVEL
CREATURES, YOU WIN!**

WHAT DO YOU WIN?

**THE RELEASE OF DREXEL
CAINE. DETAILS SOON.**

**AND IF YOU TELL ANYONE,
ANYONE, BAD THINGS WILL
HAPPEN.**

PLAY ON!

My throat feels suddenly dry and scratchy. Did Drexel really get kidnapped right from the grounds of a *spy* school? How does that even happen? Jennifer is not going to like this.

"Oh, man," I say.

"Yeah," says Toby glumly.

"When did you get it?"

"After basketball practice," he says. "My phone was in my room, locked up like always because, you know, it does things, and I don't want anyone to get hurt." When it comes to technology, Toby is a whiz. He can do anything. In fact, he used to be the Center's main man for anything tech. You know all the cool spy gear you see in the movies? That was Toby. I say "was" because now he's on the bench waiting to turn sixteen, just like me.

"Can you trace this Menace somehow?"

He shakes his head. "Tried that. Nothing. I can't find a single clue about him. Or her."

"That's comforting."

"Oh, it's way worse than that. I'm supposed to play at platinum level, but look, I have no points."

I glance back at the screen. It's true. Usually, you level up when you amass points, and you can use those points to buy information and weapons to help capture more monsters and get more points and so on. Toby is no better off than a dorky bronze-level player staggering around in the Monster Mayhem dark.

"And Menace got in the back end. He's controlling the game, which means he's pretty good." This is high praise coming from Toby.

"Is it for real?" I ask.

He shrugs. "I can't get ahold of Drexel."

"But that's not unusual, right?"

"Not really."

We should tell Jennifer. We should just march on down the hall to her office and hand her the message and step aside. But what if Menace really means the part about bad things happening if Toby tells? I wonder if they know he just told me. A good spy would already be planning the next step. I, of course, have no idea. This moment is really undermining my confidence.

"What are the six epic creatures?" I ask.

"I don't know. I can't even tell where I'm supposed to start looking because I have no points." True, but even so, no platinum-level creature would be caught dead hanging around our campus in the middle of nowhere.

"So what do we do right now?"

"Wait for the details from Menace. And keep our mouths shut. As in, don't blab to Charlotte and Izumi."

"I totally won't," I say. "I promise."

Toby eyes me skeptically. "I want to believe you."

"You can, I swear!" He still doesn't look convinced but agrees to let me know the second he hears anything new. We part ways because we have at least three hours of homework awaiting us.

Back at McKinsey House dorm, Charlotte, Izumi, and I decide all this homework would go down much easier with a pepperoni pizza. We sit on the carpet of Izumi's first-floor dorm room because Charlotte's room is too messy and my room is on the fourth floor, commonly referred to as Siberia. Books, binders, and folders are scattered around us. The pizza box balances precariously on top of Izumi's giant calculus textbook. Izumi is the first person in the history of the school to take calculus as a thirteen-year-old. That she tutors the struggling seniors is lost on no one.

Charlotte gazes at her French 3 textbook, pizza slice in hand, and asks me how much luggage I plan on bringing to Paris. Traditionally, French 2 and French 3 students do a week in Paris in the spring. The trip is an immersion into all things French, meant to give students some context for their classroom language struggle. In two days, we will be running wild in a foreign city and eating a lot of pastries. But how can I think about France when Drexel Caine is being held hostage and Toby has to play a perfect platinum-level round to *save* him? I mean, Iceman could probably do it, but for Toby it will be a stretch. Drexel might be doomed.

"I'm thinking two large suitcases and a small carry-on?" Charlotte says. "What do you think?"

I pull a second pizza slice from the box and blurt out, "My squash coach said I might be the worst player she's ever seen, and Drexel's been kidnapped by a maniac called Menace."

Izumi gasps and chokes on a bite. Charlotte gently puts her slice back in the open box. "Excuse me?" she says.

Shoot. This, after I promised I wouldn't tell. I didn't even last an hour. I clear my throat. "I knocked Ceci in the head with my racquet," I say. "She fell and twisted her ankle."

"We don't *care* about squash," Izumi says, her gaze narrowing.

"Oh, you mean the part about Drexel being kidnapped."

"Yes!" they say in unison.

"Well, during the thing this morning, you know the smoke and fake fire, I think he got himself kidnapped."

"For real?" Charlotte asks, eyes wide.

"Did you call the police? Did you tell Jennifer? Did *she* call the police?"

"That's the problem," I say. "The message said Toby wasn't supposed to tell anyone or Drexel might get hurt."

"Message?" Charlotte asks.

"It's complicated," I say.

"Did it say 'hurt' specifically?" Izumi presses.

"It said things might end badly. Isn't that kind of the same thing?"

"But Toby told you anyway," Charlotte points out.

"I forced him."

We sit for a moment, eating pizza and wondering about Toby's kidnapped father. Objectively, I understand why someone would want to kidnap him. He's really rich. He owns a lot of fancy cars and houses and he's on television and YouTube and things. But then again, it wouldn't surprise me if some lunatic were holding him hostage with a ransom of immediate access to Monster Mayhem 2.0 and maybe some extra points and a promise of green health forever and stuff.

"So what do we do?" Izumi asks finally. "We should try to convince Toby to tell Jennifer."

I shake my head. "He's going to flip out enough that you guys know. I have to leave the telling-Jennifer decision to him."

"This has disaster written all over it." Charlotte grins. "I can't wait to see what happens next."

Here's an observation about the kids at Smith. They are almost all the offspring of important rich people. Sure, there are a handful of scholarship students, but they number so few as to be statistically irrelevant. Take Charlotte. She's thirteen and has had almost every experience a person could have. Ski the Alps? Check. Visit the Galápagos sea turtles? Check. Go to the Olympics (with good seats!)? Have an audience with the president of the United States (she said it was dull)? Yes and yes. She shuffles from a six-bedroom penthouse on the Upper East Side of New York to a palatial spread in the Hamptons to a "sweet" little retreat on St. Barts to a stately old apartment in Geneva. Whenever she talks about her home life, she rolls her eyes and says, "It's all so manufactured."

A situation like Toby's almost certainly will lead to chaos and excitement, the very opposite of manufactured. This gives Charlotte a thrill. She likes the adrenaline rush of the unknown. She is always the first person to say yes.

Izumi, on the other hand, thinks things through. She sees all possible outcomes, and sometimes this is paralyzing and she finds she can't do anything. I'd like to think I'm somewhere in between my two best friends, but maybe that's just wishful thinking.

The pizza is gone. "Why don't we ever order dessert?" Izumi asks thoughtfully.

"Because they only sell pizza," Charlotte says. We have mounds of homework still awaiting our attention, but who cares about that?

"Maybe it's just a joke and Drexel took a vacation," Izumi suggests.

"Drexel? In the middle of his integrity lecture?"

"It was resilience, and you're right," says Charlotte. "Probably not a vacation. But Izumi has a point. How about he just went home because he figured school meeting was over?"

Drexel is a bad father. This is accepted as the undisputed truth. But even a bad parent would check up on his kid after an incident involving smoke and possibly fire, wouldn't he?

"That doesn't sound right," I say. "But I guess we just have to wait and see what happens next."

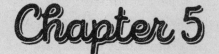

Chapter 5

WHAT HAPPENS NEXT.

WHAT HAPPENS NEXT IS Toby appears like a sweaty ghost in Izumi's window. Izumi notices first and screams. I jump and upset the pizza box, scattering rejected crusts all over the floor. Charlotte hurries to the window and drags Toby awkwardly over the sill. He lands with a thud on the floor, breathing hard. Getting to window level requires shimmying up a drainage pipe that is always on the verge of detaching from the wall, clinging to the outer edge of the window with your fingertips, and hoping someone inside notices and opens the window before you plunge to your death. Well, probably not death—it *is* only the first floor, but it's a high first floor.

"Why didn't you use the code and come in the front door?" Charlotte demands as Toby sits up, pulling a wayward pizza crust out of his hair.

"Abby said it didn't work."

"You told me that was because of user error," I bark.

"It might be because it just doesn't work." I want to kick him, but he seems miserable enough.

"I'm sorry about your dad," Izumi says.

Now I want to kick *her*.

Toby's look of surprise quickly shifts, and he glares at me. "Abby, you promised to keep your mouth shut!"

I did, and it lasted all of sixty minutes. I hang my head with shame. I can't be trusted. "Sorry," I mutter.

"You kind of had to see that coming," Izumi offers.

"Best friends don't keep secrets," Charlotte says. "Besides, it's better that we know because now we can help."

"I don't want help!" Toby shouts.

"Be quiet," Izumi hisses. "You're not supposed to be here. So what are you doing here anyway?"

Toby sits on Izumi's bed and buries his face in his hands. "I got another message," he mumbles through his fingers. We gather around him in a tight little circle.

"What does it say?" I ask. In response, he hands me his phone. It's the same home screen as before, but Toby's health is no longer green. It's yellow, which means he has to hurry up and start catching monsters, and now only a single platinum cage dangles above his head. A message bubble floats across the screen. This one is also written in all capital letters. I think Menace has a self-esteem problem.

"Read it," says Izumi.

"Capture the Quinotaur!"

"Quinotaur?" Charlotte asks.

"It's a sea monster," I say. "The translation from Latin is 'bull with five horns.' It's from French mythology." My friends stare at me. "What?"

"I'm not even going to ask how you know that," says Charlotte. "Where exactly are we supposed to capture this Quinotaur? Hopefully not Jennifer's office."

They smirk. I will never live down my Mogollon Monster fiasco.

"If only," Toby says with a sigh. Izumi swipes the phone and using her fingers, taps the cage, and zooms in on a map that is no longer blurred out.

"Nope, not the office," she says, raising an eyebrow. "This is Paris." She zooms some more. "But it won't give me any more details than that. Wait a minute. Toby, you're *bronze*? What the heck?"

"You think I didn't notice that? This is a mess." His face is still hidden in his hands, his shoulders hunched, like he's trying to disappear.

"I guess it's good we're headed to Paris," I offer. As a bronze player, Toby has to be physically close to a creature to earn more information about its actual location. Drexel said he created the game to push kids out into the world, to lead them to interesting places and get them moving. He just never imagined his life would hang in the balance. Toby keels over on the bed.

"Your health won't *last* until we get to Paris," Izumi points out. "You're low yellow right now."

Looks like someone is going to spend the night hunting werewolves out by the pond just to stay alive. I'd offer to keep him company, but I'm still recovering from my Mogollon disaster.

"I have to find out who Menace is," Toby moans. "And I can't find him from here. It's impossible. I need real computing power."

"Let's brainstorm ideas," Izumi suggests. We sit in silence for a full minute. "Well, that's not working." Toby slides to the floor in a dejected heap.

"We need a plan," I say.

"Yes, we do," Izumi says. "And that plan should be to

go and hand this whole mess to Jennifer. Who's with me?"

No one raises a hand. Izumi grimaces. "You guys are so predictable. Can I just say up front that this has trouble written all over it?"

"How do you know?"

"Are you forgetting what happened the last time?" she shouts. "People could have died!"

"But no one did," Charlotte points out.

Izumi crosses her arms against her chest defensively. "Whatever. I'm in. But I don't like it."

That's nice, but in *what*? Menace obviously knows about the school trip to Paris. I shiver. We're being watched. It's creepy.

"Toby," I say. "Focus. Where can you get enough power?"

He's still on the floor with his cheek pressed up against the empty pizza box. "DrexCon headquarters." He snorts. "But that place is a fortress. They won't even let Drexel touch anything."

"What's option two?" I ask.

"I don't know," he whines.

"There has to be something," Charlotte insists. "I thought you were, like, the Center's whiz kid. No boundary you can't cross, no wall too high, no risk too great. That kind of thing."

"They fired me," Toby says, glaring at her.

"They fired me, too," I say. "Who cares? Think!"

He pulls himself up to his knees. "Well," he says carefully, "I might be able to get in if I can use the systems down in the Catacombs."

Oh, how I wish I hadn't asked.

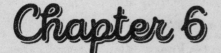

Chapter 6

THE CATACOMBS. NOT A PLACE YOU'D WANT TO VACATION.

LET ME BACK UP FOR A SECOND and fill you in on the Catacombs, because I'm sure you've already figured out we are not in ancient Greece or Rome or anyplace where real catacombs might exist. We're in Connecticut at preppy ground zero. Not the same.

In our case, Catacombs is just a fancy way of referring to the maze of subterranean, spider-infested, mostly uninhabitable space beneath the older buildings of the school. If you're caught in the Catacombs, the penalty is immediate expulsion. We are reminded of this during school meeting at least once a week.

At first I thought the school's administrators were

paranoid. What's the worst that could happen if you accidentally stumbled into the Catacombs? Were you at risk of zombie attack? Vampires? Werewolves? Surely, Tucker Harrington III, the psychotic junior bully, was scarier than anything to be found under the school, so what was everyone freaking out about? Well, turns out the Catacombs are where the spies hang out and plot and scheme and train. And they do not want you down there getting in the way or blabbing about the spy school to all your friends.

I've been down to the Catacombs a total of three times during my brief time last year as a Center spy. The official way in is through the fireplace in the headmaster's office. And in order for us to go through the fireplace, Jennifer needs to be elsewhere. I happen to know this morning during second period, when we're meant to be in the library researching topics for our Chinese History 2 presentations, Jennifer will be locked in a conference room with three visiting school trustees, thus providing the necessary window of opportunity, because there's no way Jennifer ditches the trustees. They are super-uptight rich people who arrive in limousines and smile uncomfortably when forced to eat in the school dining hall.

I have bad memories of the Catacombs, but Toby swears he needs the machines down there to break into

DrexCon. Izumi has spent the morning considering her personal limits for going where she does not belong. She's not a natural rule breaker, whereas Charlotte is downright gleeful at the prospect of finally getting into the Catacombs. We catch a break when the hallway outside the headmaster's office is empty, allowing us to unlock the door and slip in unnoticed.

Charlotte strides to the fireplace. "Should we use the Harry Potter unlocking charm? What's it called?"

"*Alohomora*, you mean?" asks Izumi.

"Come on," I say. "There's no such thing as magic. Be realistic. We're *spies*." This cracks us up. Toby stands by looking pained and waiting for our laughter to subside.

"You guys need to be serious," he says once we quiet down. "If the door code doesn't work, we're going to have to run."

And with his code-breaking track record, that's a real possibility. No one dares breathe as Toby flips open the keypad panel, hidden behind a fake stone in the fireplace surround, and punches in a sequence of numbers. My teeth automatically clench. But instead of sirens or fireballs or whatever happens when the Catacombs are compromised, the door at the back of the giant gaping fireplace yields, quietly sliding up and away to reveal the dark tunnel beyond.

"That is so cool," says Izumi, staring.

"Yeah," says Toby, but he sounds sad. I know he misses his role with the Center, and I'm still amazed he doesn't hate me for the part I played in getting him kicked out. Toby flips on a flashlight and disappears into the tunnel, followed by Charlotte and Izumi. I bring up the rear.

The tunnel, which immediately arcs down, is carved out of the rough rock that lies under the school. "Watch the low ceiling and uneven floor," I say while bumping my head and tripping over my own feet. By the time we reach the submarine-style hatch that leads to the facility below, I'm pretty sure my forehead is bloody and bruised.

The hatch seems to have gained weight in the last year, and it takes all of us to pry it open. The flashlight beam catches the ladder leading to the level below. It's enclosed in a narrow tube, kind of like a coffin. Without a word, we descend.

From the base of the ladder, it's a short walk to the Catacombs. Entering the main room for the first time makes you understand how Dorothy felt when she opened her door to find the Land of Oz outside.

The room is windowless, with a low ceiling, and painted entirely white. The automatic lights are so bright, my eyes water. On the far side of the room sits a beige sofa, a couple of chairs, and a coffee table, a cozy living room dropped into the command center of some futuristic military police force. A rectangular steel table takes up the center of the room, surrounded by eight white leather chairs. The table is empty and shiny as a mirror. On one wall are mounted nine large flat-screen monitors, organized to form a rectangle. On the opposite wall are about fifteen round clocks, labeled underneath with international destinations. At the far end of the room is another door that leads to the training rooms.

"Welcome to the command center," I say.

My friends gasp at the sight. "What is this *doing* down here?" Charlotte asks.

"Do you mean like literally or philosophically?" I ask.

"It's just so much bigger than you described it," she says.

It's weird. I get that. And it's all right here under our school. But we don't have time to ponder the big picture. We need to work fast. There's a high probability that Jennifer already knows what we're up to and is just having trouble ditching the trustees. I start to sweat.

"What's the plan, Toby?" I ask.

He tells us to stay in the main room, on lookout, while he heads to the server room, where the computers are. He doesn't tell us what we should do if someone shows up. Scream? Pretend we have amnesia and can't remember how we got down here in the first place?

I sit at the table and drum my fingers while Charlotte and Izumi roam around touching everything, like toddlers in Target. Izumi finds a stash of computer hard drives and asks if she can have them. I say no. Charlotte uncovers a box of disguises, complete with wigs, and tries on everything. I tell my friends to stop acting like tourists and stay alert.

"If someone shows up, we'll need to hide," I say.

"If someone shows up," responds Izumi, "we're dead."

She's right, of course. Where's Toby? I've never been in the server room. I've been in the training room with Veronica Brooks, my quasimentor, who kindly kicked my butt, and I've been in this room, obviously, but that's it. I wonder what Veronica would do if she were me. First, she'd tell me with an exasperated sigh that I screwed everything up already, that I should have gone directly to Jennifer, that I should be smarter and better and faster and more clever and stronger, too. After that, she might pat me on the head in a terribly condescending way. But now that

Veronica is at the Center's strategy school in Florida, I miss her. I'm not sure what that says about me.

"Stop doing that with your fingers," Charlotte demands. She wears a red curly wig and a mustache. "It's driving me crazy. Relax already, will you?"

I can't relax. Why is Toby taking so long? Maybe he's reminiscing about the good old days with his friends, the servers.

Izumi has found the rotating shelves where Toby used to keep his spy gear. She pushes a few buttons and the shelves begin to move. She stops every few seconds to examine each shelf, with a lot of *oohs* and *aahs*.

"I want this job," she says with a determined crease in her forehead. "How do I get this job? Who's doing it now?"

I have no idea who replaced Toby. I've asked and snooped and pleaded, and I still have no idea. Jennifer just reminds me that I will know everything I need to know when it's the proper time for me to know it. It's infuriating.

"Don't know."

"Well, I want it. I'm going to apply."

Everyone knows Toby and I want into the spy school, but I always assumed we were alone in this. Am I too wrapped up in myself to notice that maybe my friends have an interest as well? Have they talked about it with one another? A spiral of anxiety uncoils in my stomach. Is it because I don't know the people I love most in the world as well as I think I do?

No. It's because there are footsteps outside the door.

Chapter 7

RUN AND HIDE. BUT NOT AT THE SAME TIME.

"HIDE!" I BARK, leaping up from the table. We pile into the open closet where Charlotte found the disguises and pull the door quickly closed. It's cramped and uncomfortable. Izumi's elbow is in my spine, and my foot is practically up Charlotte's nose. "Don't move."

"I couldn't even if I wanted to," Charlotte whines.

"Shut up!" Izumi yells.

"Stop yelling," I say. "Don't even breathe."

"How are we supposed to do that? We'll die."

"Just stay really quiet, okay?"

Jennifer enters the command center. We see her

through the small gap between the door and the frame. She speaks into a headset, waving her arms around for emphasis.

"I'm having a really hard time with this scenario you guys are spinning," she says. She fiddles with one of the computers on the table, and suddenly an image of Veronica Brooks fills the nine flat screens on the wall. She's huge. It's scary.

"I've vetted the plans and resources, ma'am," Veronica says, trying hard to keep her obvious annoyance in check. "Four times." Behind her are palm trees, a beach, and beautiful blue ocean. Her hair blows in the wind. "We need your people for this mission."

"Why isn't Director Gladwell asking me herself?" Jennifer asks, narrowing her gaze.

"She's, um, a little anxious about doing that."

"Why?" Jennifer demands.

"She says you shot her once," Veronica whispers. "Accidentally."

"That was no accident," Jennifer says, arching an eyebrow. "Tell Gladwell to put on her big-girl pants and call me directly. That's the only way I allocate resources to your Bulgarian mission."

"Yes, Headmaster," Veronica says, all business. Her loyalty to Mrs. Smith is absolute. I wonder how hard it is to call Jennifer "headmaster."

"One more thing," Jennifer adds. "I noticed some unusual security activity around the Black Book on my sensors. Repeated attempts to break into it."

"We haven't detected anything down here," Veronica says with a frown.

"Probably a glitch. I'll look into it." Jennifer softens. "It's good to see you, Veronica. How is spy college treating you?"

"I miss Smith," Veronica says quietly. "But the challenges here are good for me."

They sign off, and Jennifer leaves the command center as silently as a mouse.

We fall out of the closet in a sweaty heap. "Oh my God!" Charlotte gasps. "Fresh air!"

Toby bursts through the door from the server room. "That was way too close," he says, eyes wide. *Tell me about it.* My heart pounds against my chest. I tend to stay calm in a crisis and freak out afterward, and we're not even really to the "afterward" part yet.

"Did you get it?" I ask.

Toby holds up a flash drive and grins. "Yup. Got the

electronic signature of Menace. Just need a little time to decode it."

We head back to ground level, giddy with our success. Along the way, Charlotte asks, "Hey, what do we know about this Black Book Jennifer was talking about?"

Toby's smile disappears. "It's a digital directory of everyone who works for the Center and everything the Center does," he says. "If someone gets into it, we're in trouble. But it's crazy protected, out there somewhere in cyberspace. I wouldn't even know where to start to find it. Mrs. Smith knows and obviously Jennifer. And probably some Washington, DC, big shots, but that's it."

We end up waiting twenty minutes in the fireplace for Jennifer to take a bathroom break before we can crawl out and escape. We miss the beginning of World Civilizations 2 with Mr. Miller. He gives us each a jolly smile and ten demerits. Ten! That means we will spend the weekend of Fake Prom sorting dirty socks and uniforms in the Heidi Perry Athletic Center. Gross.

But right now, we have more pressing matters, like how to break the news to Charlotte that our luggage allotment for Paris includes one carry-on suitcase. Things could get ugly.

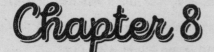

Chapter 8

PARIS. HOW ROMANTIC.

TWO DAYS LATER, we watch the adults in first class recoil in horror as thirty junior high school students stomp down the aisle toward the back of an Airbus 380 Dreamliner. Everything glows with purple light, and music plays. It's already a party.

"*Vive la France,*" Charlotte says with a grin. Not only do we get to go to Paris, but we're on a mission that is likely to be dangerous and land us in a world of trouble. Charlotte is in her happy place.

"Move it along. Keep going," urges Ms. Dunne. Her smile is tight. She might see being set on fire as an attractive alternative to chaperoning this year's French enrichment trip.

Our other chaperone, Mr. Lord, just looks annoyed. I get it. He doesn't even speak French. He was railroaded into this.

We take our seats, three across at the window. Toby sits several rows in front of us with Quinn. He's exhausted from spending every free minute trying to unravel the digital signature of whoever has taken Monster Mayhem 2.0 hostage, with little success. I don't think he's slept since we came out of the Catacombs.

From her backpack, Charlotte pulls out a satin eyeshade, fancy noise-canceling headphones, a rosewater atomizer, a small pillow, and a blanket that expands like a dry sponge dropped in a bucket of water. Izumi leans over and peers into the bag.

"What?" Charlotte asks.

"Looking for the four-poster bed," Izumi says.

Charlotte glowers at us. "I do not want to arrive in Paris puffy and tired." She sniffs. She spritzes her face and turns her back on us. We will most certainly arrive puffy *and* tired. Ms. Dunne trolls the aisles counting heads and reminding us to behave. She doesn't add "or else"—that part is understood.

"So, Abby," Izumi asks after we're cruising at forty thousand feet, "what do we do about Fake Prom?" Her face is all scrunched up with concern.

"Not go?" I suggest.

"We *have* to go."

"Why? They're just going to be mean to us."

"There's someone I want to ask," she mumbles.

"What?"

"A boy," she says. "I want to ask him to go with me."

This is a development. While Charlotte talks about liking a different boy every other day, Izumi has never mentioned one before. Ever. I thought we were in agreement that most boys are not worth the energy. Besides, we're supposed to be focused on saving Drexel right now.

"Who?" I demand.

"Parker."

"Parker Ramirez?" I don't want to sound shocked, but I can't help it. Parker, a sophomore, is the star of the Smith football team. Actually, he *is* the Smith football team. He's huge but not just physically. Parker is also superpopular and, amazingly, really nice. He's fished a number of Tucker's victims out of the Cavanaugh Family Meditative Pond and Fountain. Also, we're Middles! No one cares about us, especially superpopular, nice, humongous football-playing sophomores. I smile so she doesn't read any of this on my face.

"I know what you're thinking," she says. "I don't have a

chance. But even if I ask him and he says no, maybe we can go, and then maybe I'll see him there?"

"Maybe," I say.

"So you'll come with me?"

Wait. How did this discussion end up with me going to the Fake Prom with Izumi? What about my perfectly reasonable "not go" suggestion? But I say, "Yeah." Because that's what friends do.

Izumi gives me an awkward hug. "You're the best," she says.

During the flight, I can't sleep because now I'm going to stupid Fake Prom and I don't have an eyeshade or head-phones or a sponge blanket of my own to help. Instead, I begin to obsess over what's going to happen in Paris. Where is the Quinotaur? How will we catch it? Toby doesn't have enough points to buy a net or a stun gun or anything. He'll have to herd the Quinotaur into the cage the old-fashioned way, by waving his phone around until he virtually conks it on the head and can stuff it in the cage. And I don't think a five-horned sea monster is going to take kindly to that.

In normal life, the consequences in an augmented reality game don't really matter. So you lose some points or some health or some power. But the consequences outside the game, caused by playing it, can matter, like accidentally walking into traffic or falling in a pond or doing some-thing the French police don't like. We can't very well go wandering all over Paris, waving our phones around and hollering about Quinotaurs. Everything about this makes me uncomfortable. Toby shot down my suggestion he go to Jennifer, saying he did not want the responsibility of anything happening to Drexel. Furious I'd even brought it up, he reminded me it was just another way he could fail his father. He said he thought we were friends and I should understand. So now we're doing it Toby's way.

I finally fall into a fitful sleep somewhere over the middle of the Atlantic Ocean and dream I'm being chased by a bunch of vampires, led by *Mona Lisa*, who happens to reside in Paris. And who is also a vampire. I have to stop reading those vampire books.

Nothing misaligns the body-mind connection like crossing time zones. I've done this a lot in my life, and it never gets any easier. Logically, I know it's morning in France, but my body thinks it should still be sleeping. Charlotte, however, looks downright perky. She pokes us with a finger. I'm slumped over on Izumi, and I'm pretty sure that's a drool spot on her shoulder. Izumi opens one eye and with it conveys a world of annoyance at Charlotte, who continues to roust us from our awkward slumber.

"We're here," she says. "Wake up. It's time to take Paris!"

"Where are we taking it?" Izumi mumbles.

"You'd think," says Charlotte, "with a mother who's the ambassador to Japan, you'd be used to long flights."

"Why do you think she parked me at boarding school?" Izumi growls.

"Okay, okay. Chill."

My first instinct upon waking up is to pull out my phone, but it's parked with all the other field trip students' phones in a locked box back at Smith. The idea is you cannot become culturally enriched if you are staring at a tiny screen all the time. Before I can get too twitchy, Ms. Dunne appears in the aisle. She doesn't look perky either. "Ladies. Don't leave anything behind. And remember, only French from this point forward."

We exit the plane in a cloud of stinky morning breath and yawns. Charlotte, jumping right into this immersion thing, chats up a sour-looking immigration officer until he's smiling and blushing. He sends us through with wishes for an ecstatically wonderful trip to his beautiful country. I'd say thanks, but I can't remember that word either.

A blue bus awaits curbside to whisk us to our hotel. At the front of the bus, Ms. Dunne drones on about the rules of engagement on foreign soil—don't embarrass your parents, your teachers, your school, or your country, not necessarily in that order. She tells us she has a direct communication link to Headmaster Hunter and can basically beam reports of bad behavior right into my mother's brain. Is this enough of a deterrent to keep thirty teenagers from running amok in an exotic foreign city? We will see about that.

As the bus bounces toward our hotel, Toby slips into the empty seat beside me, his eyes wide.

"Look," he says. From his inside pocket, he pulls a disposable cell phone, a burner. The penalty for having electronics when you aren't supposed to is the loss of all weekend privileges, a million demerits, and possible expulsion, depending on the headmaster's mood. But it's not like we have much choice. On-screen, I see Toby's health is perilously low despite his bagging a few werewolves the other night. But that's not why he's freaking. From the map, it appears the Quinotaur has made itself comfortable right underneath the *Mona Lisa*.

Chapter 9

JUST THE *MONA LISA* AND US.

I PANIC RIGHT AWAY. The *Mona Lisa* is only the most well-guarded famous painting in the entire world. Creating a scene in the *Mona Lisa* room is bound to get us arrested. Is Menace using us to perpetrate an art heist? Art theft would be leveling up in a way I'm not so interested in. My heart squeezes in my chest. This is getting much too real.

"Bad," I say. "Really bad. How do we sneak off to the Louvre without getting caught? And you don't have a stun gun or a cage extender or *anything*, and there's no way we can get close enough if the Quinotaur is under the painting. Are you kidding me?"

"We need to think," Toby says, sweat breaking out on his forehead. "And fast."

Our fast thinking is interrupted when the bus pulls to a stop in front of the Grand Hotel, located on the Champs-Elysées. As the name suggests, it's grand, much more so than we deserve except that Charlotte's father owns a piece of this hotel chain, so here we are, wrapped in luxury at a discounted rate. Boys' rooms are in A Tower, and girls' are in B Tower. The towers have separate elevator banks, meaning if you plan to sneak from one to the other, you have to traipse across the very large and open lobby. And the lobby is monitored by cameras and humans twenty-four hours a day. Ms. Dunne mentions this two or three times.

She also mentions that after we check in and get settled, we will go directly to the Louvre for a private viewing of the *Mona Lisa*. Toby stares at me, and I stare back. I don't believe in coincidences. Here's that creepy being-watched feeling again.

As Ms. Dunne rattles on about how viewing the world's most famous painting privately is a privilege to be savored, I quickly fill Izumi and Charlotte in on developments. I tune back in just as Ms. Dunne reminds us yet again to be impressed.

We're not. We're grumpy. We mill around the grand lobby, jet-lagged and hungry, as Mrs. Dunne sorts through paperwork and gets room assignments. My friends slump over like deflated balloons in a few deep lounge chairs. Going for a private viewing of the *Mona Lisa* may be a privilege, but from the looks of this crowd, they are not going to appreciate it. Someone is going to cry.

I'm lost in this thought, listening to Izumi snore, when I notice a boy in the corner of the lobby in an ugly plaid beret, too large for his head and awkward rather than jaunty. Half hidden by shadow, he watches us intently.

I keep my eyes on him as we finally disperse to our towers. I'm not cynical about people, just suspicious. Bad Beret waits for a moment before trailing after Toby, Quinn, and the other boys to A Tower.

Of course, I have to follow him. That's a given.

"Can you guys take my bag?" I say, shoving my roll-aboard suitcase at Charlotte. "I have to go see something." Without giving her time to object, I take off after Bad Beret. But my timing is not so good, and I end up in the elevator with him. To avoid suspicion, I pretend to be hyperabsorbed in the ceiling tiles.

"What floor?" he asks, and for the first time I get a look at him. He's a wiry teenager, about our age, with acne blemishes on his olive cheeks and little round glasses.

"Um," I stammer. "Six?" He presses six for me and seven for himself. When the elevator spits me out on the sixth floor, I race for the stairs. I pop out on the seventh floor just in time to see the hat disappear around the corner.

I follow, lurching to a halt when the boy stops in front of Toby's room. He glances both ways to make sure no one is watching and raises his hand to knock. But something stops him. His shoulders slide up to his ears as if he's fighting a rising fury inside his chest. Hearing commotion behind the door, he drops his hand and walks quickly away.

Toby, Quinn, and a boy named Augustus Weaver III tumble out of the room. They're laughing and punching one another and tripping over their own feet. Auggie sprawls flat on his face on the dark patterned carpet. They talk in friend shorthand, blathering on about some video game. You'd never suspect what Toby is carrying around with him. My heart squeezes at how brave he is.

From where I crouch, I can see Bad Beret. He watches the boys, his eyes bright and agitated, his hands clenched in tight fists. Etched on his face is an expression of pure envy. It's hard to look at, like catching someone in a moment expected to be private. As Toby and his posse disappear from view, raw pain and anger replace envy. I want to look away, but my eyes are glued to his face. What happened to this boy in the bad beret? Whatever it is, it's bad. I slink away as soon as I can.

As I pass through the lobby, I ask the front desk for my room number. Or maybe I ask "Where is my potato?" Either way, it takes a few tries to figure out where I'm going. And I finally get there only to discover Charlotte and Izumi, fully clothed, squished in the empty bathtub and deep in conversation.

"What are you guys doing?" I ask, because clearly someone has to.

"We're talking about Parker and Fake Prom," Charlotte says. "It's right when we get back. We don't have much time."

"We're strategizing," Izumi adds. "Want to join us?"

I sit on the ledge of the tub.

"Charlotte says you'll be my Fake Prom standby," Izumi says, matter-of-factly, "in case Parker doesn't go for it."

Gee, am I supposed to say thank you? "What about Charlotte?" I ask. "Why can't she be the standby?"

They both look at me like I just suggested *we* steal the *Mona Lisa*. "Because I'll have a date, silly," Charlotte says. *Great.*

"Can we change topics for a second?" I ask. "Did you

guys happen to see a boy in the lobby? He was wearing a beret."

Izumi is wedged awkwardly under the faucet. "Did you follow someone? Is that where you went?"

I tell them about Bad Beret and how he looked watching Toby. They tell me he probably works for the hotel. They tell me I'm jumping at shadows and blame it on the jet lag. I tell them I don't get jet-lagged. They tell me not to mention Bad Beret to Toby because he's already freaked out enough about *Mona Lisa*. I tell them we should *all* be freaked out about *Mona Lisa*. They roll their eyes, reminding me that Toby has caught hundreds of monsters. Why should the Quinotaur be any different? Then we get out of the tub because we're now five minutes late for meeting in the lobby. We race downstairs and slide in around the edges of the group, hoping not to be noticed.

A steady rain falls. We shuffle onto the bus. Within minutes, I'm the only one awake. From the outside, the Louvre looks like a palace fit for a king, which it was until 1793, when it became the world's largest museum, covering almost eight million square feet and holding over thirty-five thousand artworks. That's a lot of art.

In the huge center courtyard, a glass pyramid rises as if from the sands of Egypt. It looks out of place next to the old building, but that might be the point. The bus turns up from the Quai François Mitterrand, the Seine behind us, and pulls curbside in front the museum. There are several gasps from my classmates. For the uninitiated, the experience of the Louvre, before even taking a step inside, is pretty awesome.

As we gather in the courtyard, Ms. Dunne unfurls a red flag attached to an extendable pole. She waves it above her head with vigor. I can only guess she intends to carry this flag as we snake through the museum so we don't get lost. How mortifying.

"Remember your manners," she shouts to our group in French, "and don't get lost!" We follow the perky red flag into the glass pyramid, through the admission gates, and into the museum. I elbow Toby to get an updated countdown because at platinum level he has to play against the clock. Three hours. We got this. No problem.

Immediately upon entering the museum, at least ten kids disappear. Mr. Lord is dispatched to chase after them. Ms. Dunne pushes forward, flag flying, a pirate embarking on a journey almost certain to end in embarrassment. Thirty kids in the biggest museum in the world. What could possibly go wrong?

Chapter 10

THIS AGAIN?

AN ENTHUSIASTIC FRENCH DOCENT, Marie-Claire, who speaks a mile a minute, joins us. She must think we all have a Charlotte-level handle on French, but that's a mistake. Charlotte is a genius when it comes to languages. She learned Mandarin from an app. The rest of us are mostly to be pitied. Marie-Claire says what a special treat it is to have a closed viewing of the *Mona Lisa* and how this is quite rare indeed. She's going through the rules, and there are a lot of them, when I catch just a glimpse of a familiar beret, slipping around a corner up ahead.

Bad Beret Boy followed us here? This is not a good development. I understand why Charlotte and Izumi didn't want me to tell Toby about Bad Beret, but I think I have to. We trail after Ms. Dunne's red flag toward the Denon Wing of the museum. I fall in beside Toby. His eyes dart every which way.

"Hey," I whisper.

"Hey yourself," he says, his face pinched. "Look at this." According to Monster Mayhem, Toby will have to get right next to the *Mona Lisa* to capture the Quinotaur. Right *next* to it. And that is simply not possible, private viewing or not.

"Toby and Abby," Ms. Dunne barks. "Quiet!"

"I have to tell you something," I say quickly.

"After the bathroom," he says, shoving his jacket at me. "Hold this. Be back in a second." Toby slips away. The crowd closes in his wake. Up front, Marie-Claire talks about *Mona Lisa*'s enigmatic smile, how many times she's been stolen, and some other things that I can't understand. Charlotte is at the front of our group, eagerly soaking up Marie-Claire's every beautifully accented word. By the time we leave here, she will be able to mimic our docent perfectly.

Many people come to the Louvre for a lightning tour of its greatest hits: *Mona Lisa*, Winged Victory, Venus de Milo, the Regent diamond, a painting called *Liberty Leading the People*, and a handful of Vermeers. Because of their popularity, the museum makes these pieces of art easy to find. We move straight ahead into the home of *Mona Lisa*, room six, a cavernous space once used for legislative sessions presided over by Napoleon Bonaparte. I wonder if he stood on a stool at the front of the room so everyone could see him. The walls are cream-colored and the parquet floors an intricate crisscross of pale wood. Overhead, diffuse light rains down as if from the heavens above. Behind us, the massive wooden door swings closed, ensuring no one interrupts our private session.

There are other paintings in this gallery, but they are the ugly stepsisters. At the far end is the *Mona Lisa*, behind a sealed enclosure, protected by an inch and a half of bulletproof glass. The enclosure is temperature-controlled and wobble-proof, so even if an unexpected earthquake gobbled up France, the *Mona Lisa* would survive.

I can't help think she looks lonely up there and so small against the large, otherwise empty wall. She's the girl no one is allowed to play with, too special for her own good, eating alone in the cafeteria. More important, there is no way for Toby to get physically close enough to catch the Quinotaur. It's an impossible task.

This is what I'm thinking when suddenly we're plunged into a nightmare of flashing red lights and wailing sirens. Naturally, everyone freaks. The guards bellow in French, which helps us not at all.

Under the noise is the grinding of steel doors sliding into place, protecting the artwork. The screaming starts as soon as the cold water begins to rain down from the sprinkler system. This cannot happen again! Marie-Claire yells for calm and runs around in panicked circles. Ms. Dunne races to the gallery doors and pulls fruitlessly on the handles, her red flag limp and dripping.

I grab Izumi and hang on. Charlotte plows into us as if thrown from across the room.

"What's going on?" she yells.

Before I can answer, an invisible hand grabs for Toby's jacket. When I don't let go, I'm dragged from the wall and swallowed by a crowd of students moving like zombies, arms out, bumping into one another in the darkness. I can't see who's got the other end of the jacket in the flashing red light, but I'm not letting go. I wrap the sleeve around my arm and dig in my heels. But this does nothing to stop my slide across the slippery floor. I trip over something that might be a backpack or a student crouched low, and sprawl headlong onto the ground. My knees hit hard, and I barely have time to get an arm out to keep my face from smacking the wood floor. But I don't let go of the jacket.

"Give it to me," growls a voice very near to my ear. "Now." Bad Beret! He snakes an arm around my throat and squeezes. I struggle to hold on to the jacket and not pass out.

In my back pocket, I have a pencil with which I'm supposed to write down important facts about Italian Renaissance art. Instead, I pull it out and bury it deep in Bad Beret's arm. He howls, the agony drowned out almost completely by the sirens. I scramble away on hands and knees, keeping low, dragging the soaked jacket behind me.

We hear heavy pounding from the other side of the gallery doors before they burst open. Light pours in along with about twenty armed guards. They spread out to the four corners of the room, yelling and throwing weird hand signals at each other. I scan the room for Bad Beret, but he's gone. Any blood on the floor is washed clean by the water. I duck out of the way as four guards, weapons drawn, march into position in front of the *Mona Lisa* enclosure, now dripping with water.

She's still there, in case you were wondering. Still smiling down on us mysteriously, benevolently. If she knows what this is all about, she's not saying.

Several guards cordon us off in a space near the door.

The sprinklers stop, but we're already soaked through and miserable. Ms. Dunne demands an explanation while Mr. Lord, slightly dazed, repeatedly wipes the water from his eyes. After a while, a man enters the gallery. He's dressed in a suit and has an official look about him, right down to his very tidy mustache.

"Chief Inspector Durand," he says, eyeballing our wet lot distastefully. "I will need to know if you saw anything suspicious."

Something about the way he delivers this line makes Charlotte giggle. Within seconds, the laughter spreads like a virus, and Chief Inspector Durand is faced with a pack of overtired, uncomfortable, cackling hyenas. Ms. Dunne tries in vain to shut us up, but it's pointless. The inspector stomps his foot to get our attention, but this makes things worse. So he does what he must. He waits for us to stop. Finally, the laughter dies down.

"Please report anything you saw," he says. An eerie silence settles in. I think of Bad Beret. Do I tell the inspector? I scan the group quickly, trying to pick Toby's dark curls out of the crowd. I can't say anything without Toby's consent. This is his mission.

But Toby isn't here.

I tug on Izumi's sleeve. "Where's Toby?"

She glances around. "Don't know."

"No one saw anything unusual?" Durand asks. "Nothing?"

I raise my hand. "Mademoiselle?"

"Toby Caine," I say.

"This Toby is unusual?" Durand asks.

"Abby," Ms. Dunne says hotly, "whatever you're up to, now is not the time."

"I'm not up to anything," I protest. "And Toby isn't unusual, but he is missing. He never came back from the bathroom."

Chapter 11

ALWAYS CHECK THE POCKETS.

THERE'S ABOUT A HALF HOUR of chaos, during which time it is confirmed that Toby is not in any of the bathrooms nor anywhere in the Louvre and is therefore indeed missing. If they'd believed me at the start, we'd be thirty minutes closer to finding him, I'm just saying. But instead of staying on the task of finding the missing student, Durand and his buddies question us in depth about some gift shop thefts when we didn't even have time to go shopping.

Ms. Dunne and Mr. Lord try to remain calm and do a pretty good job, except when Ms. Dunne has to inform Headmaster Hunter that she lost a student. She turns all white and looks like she might faint right into the arms of

Detective Inspector Durand, who hovers nearby.

Izumi, Charlotte, and I get our own special questioning.

Durand: "You are friends with this missing student?"

Izumi: "Yes. I guess. Not that he makes it easy all the time. Right?"

Charlotte: "I don't think Monsieur Durand cares about that."

Izumi: "It's true, though. He's moody."

Charlotte: "So are you!"

Me: "Most teenagers are moody."

Durand: "Quiet, please! Do you know where he went?"

Me: "He wouldn't go anywhere on purpose without his jacket."

Durand: *"Pourquoi?"*

Charlotte: "It's a hate gift from his dad."

At this point, Durand looks around frantically for reinforcements, specifically someone who speaks American Teenager. But he's alone. The fear is obvious in his twitchy eyebrows.

Charlotte: "It's a custom-made Belstaff. That's a British company. Four thousand dollars."

Izumi: "So around thirty-five hundred euros."

Durand (more eyebrows): "Thank you, mademoiselle."

Izumi: "You're welcome."

Charlotte: "Would you like to hear more about the jacket?"

Durand: "No. Please. No more about the jacket."

Ms. Dunne appears. Inspector Durand pleads with her to help, and she gladly rescues him.

Dunne: "The inspector would like to know if you have any information on Toby. And I'd like to know as well. Is this some plot you guys cooked up to derail this trip?"

Charlotte: "Of course not!"

Izumi: "If they did, I was not informed."

Me: "We didn't. And that's the truth."

Dunne: "Abby, your record with the truth is not so great."

Charlotte: "Toby couldn't just vanish into thin air. He has to be somewhere. Who pulled the alarm? That's what I want to know. Do you suspect Toby?"

Durand: "The video of the alarm puller is . . . compromised."

Izumi: "So do you mean your machine wasn't recording or someone erased it?"

Charlotte: "I'd bang some heads if my guards forgot to turn on the surveillance cameras."

Me: "Poor-quality work, for sure."

Durand: "My American friends, please stop talking. Please. I beg you."

It goes downhill from there.

After an hour, we are released back to our bus with a frazzled Mr. Lord and an oddly serene Ms. Dunne. Charlotte imagines this has something to do with the detective inspector and his "request" that Ms. Dunne join him for coffee later. Just to talk about the case of the missing student, of course. Charlotte is an Olympic-level eavesdropper.

Back in our room, under strict orders to stay put until the Toby thing is sorted, we climb into the tub for a discussion. I ask for theories.

"The alarm was a diversion," Izumi says. "So Toby could get the Quinotaur. He did it. And somehow compromised the tape."

We take a moment to recognize the potential magnitude of Toby's actions.

"Hard-core," whispers Charlotte with admiration.

But while I'm impressed with his ability to pull a fast one in a museum with world-class security, I still don't know where he is. And why he didn't tell us what he was going to do. "But why disappear afterward if no one saw you?" I ask.

"Do you know the penalty for locking down the *Mona Lisa* room?" Izumi asks.

"No."

"Me either, but I bet it's huge."

"Maybe he got more instructions once he caught the Quinotaur and had to act fast?" Charlotte offers.

"That would be, like, light speed fast," Izumi says.

"How about he's been kidnapped by the kidnappers?"

"Maybe he ran away. Couldn't take the pressure and snapped."

I hold up a hand for them to stop. "Okay. Enough. What about the jacket?" I ask. "Why did Bad Beret want it?"

We stare at the sodden, misshapen jacket as it hangs over the edge of the giant tub. The leather is dark and water-stained and sad. "You know what?" Izumi asks.

"Yes," Charlotte and I say at the same time. We have yet to search the jacket. We are lousy spies.

I haul the jacket into the tub with us. Zipped into an inside pocket is the flash drive Toby used in the Catacombs and a folded brochure, mushy and wet. I gingerly smooth it out on the tile floor.

"The Château de Versailles," Charlotte says, examining it. "It's the tourist map."

On the brochure cover, the sand-colored stone of the enormous sprawling palace stands in sharp relief against a perfect blue sky and crisp green gardens. It looks so serene it's hard to imagine that in 1789 an angry mob drove out

King Louis XVI and Marie Antoinette, an event that eventually led to them losing their heads. Literally.

Izumi tentatively picks up the damp paper and flips it over. Across the back, scrawled in block letters, it says, *ICEMAN FRIDAY 10AM BY THE CONES.*

"Iceman!" we shriek in unison. The evil villain who dominates the Monster leaderboard.

"Did he tell you about this?" Charlotte asks, indignant.

I shake my head. It seems he doesn't tell me anything. My chest goes tight with anger.

"This is getting too complicated," Izumi says. "I think we need to tell. Toby could be in real danger. Iceman is not to be messed with."

I get that. I really do. But at the same time, I *promised* him I wouldn't say anything to anyone. Yes, I immediately broke this promise and told my best friends, but they don't count. Plus, wouldn't it be better if we knew what we were dealing with first? Wouldn't Jennifer be impressed if we handed her actual intelligence on Menace *and* Iceman? There's even the possibility they waive the rule of being sixteen because we prove ourselves to be that good.

Charlotte eyeballs me. "I know what you're thinking, and I'm in."

Izumi says, "No way. Forget it."

"I promise if we learn anything, we'll tell Ms. Dunne or Jennifer immediately." This sounds reasonable if you disregard the breaking-of-all-Ms.-Dunne's-rules-in-order-to-make-it-happen part.

"This is a bad idea," Izumi says.

"It's not her first bad idea," Charlotte points out.

"Thanks," I say. "Izumi, you don't have to come. It's probably way too risky and completely stupid and—"

"Okay, okay! You guys are my only friends, so *oui*, yes, I'm in, but only if you promise to tell Jennifer everything. And not get us killed. Or arrested. Or tossed in some black site prison in Romania. Or let my mom find out. *Très bien?*"

"*D'accord*," I say.

"*Oh mon Dieu*," says Charlotte, sounding exactly like Marie-Claire. "*Votre français est tragique.*"

Chapter 12

A SIDE TRIP FROM THE FIELD TRIP.

THE BEST WAY TO GET to the Palace of Versailles is by train. Take the RER C, get off at the last stop, and walk five minutes. Easy. The hard part is escaping the clutches of Ms. Dunne and Mr. Lord, who have become very clingy. Last night we were informed that Toby was perfectly safe. They offered no details, and requests were summarily denied. But if Toby is safe, why do they still seem so strung out? This is just further evidence we need to find out what is going on.

In the chic hotel bistro, we eat croissants for breakfast and drink multiple café au laits because they are delicious and we aren't allowed to drink them at Smith. All this coffee leads to extreme hyperactivity, which is almost more than Ms. Dunne and Mr. Lord can handle. I swear there's a sprinkling of new white hair in Mr. Lord's dark brown sideburns. I'd feel sorry for my teachers, but I don't have time. I'm plotting a jailbreak.

On the morning's agenda is a visit to the Arc de Triomphe, one of Paris's most famous monuments honoring the soldiers who died in the French Revolution and the Napoleonic Wars. I've already been to the Arc, so I don't feel like I'm leaving a giant hole in my cultural résumé by bailing. We decide to use the oldest scam in the book: fake an illness. We vote for Charlotte to act the part of the sick student, and she graciously accepts. Izumi and I will play concerned best friends, willing to sacrifice our day to sit bedside with our ill classmate.

We choose right after breakfast, before boarding the bus. In the lobby of the Grand Hotel, Charlotte suddenly grabs her stomach, drops to her knees, and makes the most awful retching sounds. She moans and goes a shade pale. How does she do that? It's amazing. If I didn't know better, I'd be freaking out. Exactly how Ms. Dunne is, for example.

"Oh, my dear," she says, bending down by Charlotte. "Are you okay? What's the matter?"

Charlotte's forehead beads with sweat. Her eyes roll

back in her head. If she takes this any further, she's going to end up in the hospital, and that will be a real problem. I make a slashing motion at my throat. Charlotte grips Ms. Dunne's arm and says in a faint voice, "I think I ate something that didn't agree with me. I might need to lie down. I'm sure I'll be fine in a few hours."

Izumi giggles. I stomp on her foot. Ms. Dunne helps Charlotte stand up, keeping a firm grip as if afraid she, too, might suddenly vanish. Mr. Lord stands by, wringing his hands. Charlotte takes a dramatic seat on a lobby chair while a fretful Ms. Dunne confers with Mr. Lord. This is our moment. Izumi and I rush in.

"We can stay with her," I say. "We'll bring her back to the room and let her rest. We can catch up with you when she's feeling better. I'm sure her father, who got us the hotel, would appreciate her not being left alone when she's unwell."

Ms. Dunne furrows her eyebrows. She's no dunce, and if she weren't so stressed out right now she'd see clear through our ruse. But in the last twenty-four hours, she's been in a museum lockdown and lost a student. She's way off her game.

She rolls back on her heels. "I'm going to call to check in every hour," she says, pointing a finger in my face. "And you'd *better* be there."

"Where else would we be?" Izumi asks.

Charlotte gives a little moan. "I'd be *so* much happier lying down," she whispers.

We each take an arm and slowly walk Charlotte to the elevator banks. "Every hour!" Ms. Dunne calls after us.

"Got it!" I yell back.

"That was barely even a challenge," says Charlotte, disappointed.

"Still," says Izumi, "you were pretty good. Especially the gasping and moaning."

"You don't think it was too much?" Charlotte asks. Feedback on one's performance is necessary for improvement.

"You were right on the line," I offer. "Could have gone south in a heartbeat."

Now that we're out of view, Charlotte straightens up. "You're very critical." She sniffs.

Back in the room, we throw a few necessary items into my backpack: M&M's, water bottle, map of Paris because all our cell phones are locked in a safe in Ms. Dunne's hotel room (except for Toby's because they don't know he has seven), gum, a hairbrush (Charlotte), lip balm (Charlotte), calculus textbook (Izumi—in case there's a train delay), and the brochure for Versailles. Outside, a steady drizzle falls, so we add an umbrella.

For cover, we use a nail file to fray the wall connection of the phone. If the phone doesn't work, we have an excuse for not answering it. Now we just need to be back in this room by the time the tour of the Arc is over. No problem.

Although Ms. Dunne did not specifically say the front desk would be on the lookout for us, we hedge our bets and leave the back way through the kitchen. We get a lot of strange looks, but if you pretend nothing is out of the ordinary you are soon forgotten.

We pop into a back alley and, huddled under our single umbrella, immediately head in the wrong direction. We figure this out after about three blocks, turn around, and head for the Metro. Charlotte waltzes through the Paris Metro like I do the New York City subway. No one gives us a second glance. Soon we're on the RER C, which smells like wet dog, headed for Versailles.

As the train rattles toward our destination, I have a few moments to reflect on what we're doing. Inevitably, we're going to get busted. And Ms. Dunne is going to freak. And Jennifer is going to kill me. This is generally what adults mean when they waggle their eyebrows at you and speak of "poor choices."

"Can I apologize in advance for whatever happens?" I ask.

Izumi glances up from the Paris and Surrounding Areas map. "Sure," she says. "I guess."

Charlotte twists her blond hair into perfect ringlets and stares out the window. "Don't apologize," she says. "Own it." Easy for her to say.

The train reaches the last stop, and we disembark with a few intrepid sneaker-clad tourists. It's about a five-minute walk to the palace, leaving us roughly twenty minutes to case the location of the meeting. I'm a little nervous. Why on earth was Toby meeting with Iceman? I turn the flash drive over and over in my pocket.

We arrive at the palace ticket window. The dreary weather has kept the crowds at bay, so we sail right in. There are some big houses in New York, but this is ridiculous. We quickly learn Versailles has seven hundred rooms, more than two thousand windows, twelve hundred and fifty chimneys, and sixty-seven staircases. I would not want to clean this place. Izumi points out that the estate is over two thousand acres, two hundred and thirty of which are manicured gardens. How do we find "cones" by ten o'clock if we don't even know what we're looking for? We don't, that's how.

Izumi, who is systematic in almost all things except for rugby, which she says must be played from the heart, sees my face collapse. She glances at her watch.

"We don't have much time," she says, studying a map of Versailles. "If you wanted to have a secret meeting, you'd probably not want to do it inside because of the guards." That's true. There are a lot of guards in here, and I swear they all stare at us. I smile sweetly. This has no discernible effect. I should leave the charming of French people to Charlotte. "So do we take a leap and say that whatever 'cones' means it'll be somewhere outside in the gardens?"

Izumi's leap cuts off seven hundred possible rooms where this meeting might take place. But she's right. We can't search the entire palace and the grounds in twenty minutes. "Yes," I say with a confidence I don't feel. Failure is coming up fast. I see it barreling down the tracks right toward us.

We follow Izumi as she leads us out of the opulence and into the splendor. Actually, the gardens aren't so splendid because it's gray and wet, but I will give them expansive. They spread from the palace toward the horizon, as far as the eye can see. Wide pathways meander around reflecting pools and ornate statues. We stand on the wide steps of the palace and survey the scene.

"This is a big backyard," says Charlotte.

It's also a catastrophe. "How are we supposed to find

anything out here?" I moan. An eerie silence hangs over the gardens. We are the only ones outside.

"Cones," says Izumi. As if we need reminding.

"Maybe the cones are a painting?" I say. "Or a sculpture?"

"Or maybe the little ones they put out by bathrooms when they're cleaning them?" says Charlotte.

"Do they even do that in France?" I ask.

"I don't know," says Charlotte with a shrug.

"Cones," says Izumi again.

"I know," responds Charlotte impatiently, "but what does that *even* mean?"

"You guys are super-dense." Izumi points. We follow her direction and there on the far side of a rectangular reflecting pool are a series of pine trees, all shaped exactly like giant orange safety cones.

Chapter 13

SO WHO IS THIS ICEMAN ANYWAY?

IT IS 9:58. We run for the cone-shaped pine trees. Subtle, I know. There are twelve of them, spaced about ten feet apart. Planted parallel is another row of trees, round ones this time and in enormous ceramic containers. Together they create a narrow path, heavily shaded and almost dark from the tree cover. We fan out and begin to walk the distance of the tree rows. Izumi is on the outside of the cone trees, I'm on the path in between, and Charlotte is on the round tree side. I can barely see them as we quickly move the length of the tree rows. Nothing. No sign of anything out of the ordinary. We regroup at the far side.

"Now what?" Izumi asks.

"We wait?" I suggest.

"Again, I think we really need to work on our planning," Charlotte says. "We keep ending up like this."

"Okay," I say, annoyed. "I appoint you head of the planning department."

"No need to get snippy about it," she says.

"I'm not!" I protest.

"You are," she says.

"Can you guys stop?" Izumi pleads. "This is serious. This is *Iceman*. Our lives are probably in grave danger right now."

As if to prove Izumi right, suddenly giant frying-pan-size hands grab me from behind and pull me around the back of a cone tree. The hands wedge a gag in my mouth. Out of the corner of my eye, I see my friends have been grabbed in a similar fashion. My kidnapper has me in a human straitjacket. The backpack is squished between us, Izumi's calculus book stabbing me in the spine. This is just as I imagined Iceman to be. Huge. Terrifying. Powerful. I crane my neck around for a glimpse of the mask. It's a garden-variety bank-robber kind, black with no distinguishing marks. This was not a good idea. Why did I think this Iceman would just show up and be willing to have a nice chat with us? He's a notorious criminal! I'd kick myself, but I can't even do that right. Iceman drags me deeper into the gardens to a green hedgerow maze with patches of ground fog to make it more sinister because that's what I need right now. Remember when Harry Potter went into the maze? Bad things happened.

I struggle, and Iceman's grip grows tighter.

"Let me go," I say. It comes out garbled because of the gag. I wiggle my jaw, trying to dislodge it, but it's too tight. My feet drag along the sandy pathway, little stones filling my wet sneakers. We're moving too fast for me to get my feet flat on the ground. I hammer an elbow into the guy's kidneys, but it's like smashing a brick wall. My elbow throbs instantly. In the distance, I hear Izumi calling for Charlotte and me. She must have gotten free.

I don't panic. Sure, being taken hostage at Versailles is not the best thing that could happen—I mean, look how it ended for Marie Antoinette—but I've been in worse situations. Haven't I? What to do next should be my point of focus. Hmmm. I have no idea. Charlotte's right. I need to work on my planning. When meddling, one should always have a contingency plan. I don't have one of those. If I could get the gag out of my mouth, I could at least ask what he wants.

"This would be easier if you'd stop, like, moving all

around," Iceman says. From his statement, I deduce two things. He's not French and he has a cold.

"Grr . . . um . . . shum . . . berg," I say.

"What? Listen, I'm not feeling my best, so don't give me a hard time."

This is the legendary Iceman? I have to say I'm a tad disappointed.

"Grr . . . um . . . shum . . . berg!"

"You want me to take off the gag?"

I nod vigorously. We stop in a section of the maze totally enclosed by tall shrubs. A layer of mist settles over us. "Oh," he says. "I don't think so. I'm not supposed to." He sneezes all over my head. Gross.

"Shmease?" I say. He holds me out a few inches and studies me. His eyes are watery blue and shifty. I try to look harmless. Mostly, I *am* harmless. I learned last year that I'm not a natural talent at martial arts and I really hate being hit. The man removes the gag. I inhale deeply the cool, damp air.

"Thank you," I say. We stand facing each other. Iceman might also be nicknamed Mountain Man—he's definitely the right size. I have several options. I could run, but I don't think I'll get far enough to make it worthwhile. I could scream, but that might result in the gag going back in my mouth. Or I could wait for an opening, grab the sharp gardening trowel left on the ground along the hedgerow, and whack him with it. I like the sound of that. Now I just need the opening.

"No problemo," says Iceman. Tufts of bleached blond hair escape from the bottom of the ski mask. It's cold and raining, but on his tan feet, he wears grungy flip-flops and sports a silver toe ring.

He's got to be from California. Or Hawaii. Maybe that means he's laid-back. And I can use this to my advantage.

"Do I need to zip-tie your hands?" he asks.

"No," I say. Does anyone ever answer "yes" to that question? "Are you a surfer? I mean, in your spare time?"

"Dude!" He high-fives me. "Totally."

"Can you tell me what's going on?" I ask politely.

"We're waiting on Iceman," he explains.

Wait a minute. "You're not Iceman?" I ask.

He cracks up, snorting and laughing. "Oh man, no way. Not even close."

Suddenly, I shiver, and not necessarily from the temperature. "And when can we expect Iceman?"

"The Iceman comes when the Iceman comes," he says with a sigh.

"And my friends?"

"They're fine." His eyes drift here and there. He scratches his face through the ski mask like he has fleas. He whistles a little, hums a little. I know what's happening. I've seen it before, most recently in Chemistry for Beginners with Mr. Joseph. In the three minutes we've been standing here, Mountain Man has traveled from on task to thoroughly bored. This is my opening.

"What's your favorite break?" I ask. I heard this term once in a surfing movie. I have no idea if I'm using it correctly, but Mountain Man's eyes light up.

"Mavericks, baby," he says reverently. "I'm a big wave surfer."

"Wow." I try to look dazzled as I take a small step toward the trowel.

"Yeah. Right? Totally!" He gazes into space, reliving his best days on the water.

"Yeah!" I say, sliding forward. "Right. Totally. Awesome. Do you ever fall?"

"Never," he says. "Well, once, but that was so not my fault. That was some dude who was a total newbie and stole my line and I did it to save his life."

"You're a good person," I say. I'm so close. I can almost touch the trowel with my toe.

"Do you have any other hobbies?" I ask. "I mean, to fill

the time when you're not, you know, out here doing this?"

"Hey," he says, suddenly serious. I go for inconspicuous. Just hanging around here, being a good captive. "I only do this for the money. Iceman pays. I don't know where it comes from and I don't want to know. I just do what I'm told and that helps me with the bills."

"I get it," I say. I don't mention there are plenty of other ways to earn a living that don't involve kidnapping girls on behalf of some mysterious criminal element. But I worry the concept might tax my surfer friend's intellectual capacity. He's a human ostrich. Very large body. Small brain.

Done justifying himself, he drifts off again. I lunge for the shovel, intent on swinging it up and right into his face. But in the split second before the shovel makes contact, someone appears from around a hedge.

"I wouldn't do that if I were you."

Iceman.

Chapter 14

ASSUMPTIONS MAKE YOU LOOK STUPID.

A GOOD SPY SHOULD never assume anything. She should know that things are seldom as they seem. Imagine how I feel upon seeing that Iceman isn't a man at all but rather a girl, probably a year or two older than me. Her dripping rain jacket only partially obscures a pink satin party dress tied with a bedazzled sash. Her thick dark hair is swept up under a cute fedora. She wears black Converse high-tops laced all the way up. My hand freezes in midair. Mountain Man snaps to it, grabs the trowel, and shoves me back on my heels.

"Oh please, relax," she tells Mountain Man in accented English. "I'm sure our guest means you no harm. You don't, do you?" I shake my head. "See? Wonderful." She has a stillness about her that's unsettling. She studies me like a child peering into the lemur cage at the zoo.

"*Parlez-vous français?*" she asks.

"Badly," I say.

"You Americans," she mutters. "So pathetically mono-lingual. English hurts my tongue. I can easily do Arabic, Berber, Spanish, or French, but no. It has to be English. Check her pack." She waves a hand toward Mountain Man. Her nails are painted bright red, and they clash with her pink dress. I get the sense this is not something she's concerned about. Mountain Man wrenches off my backpack and dumps the contents into a puddle. Out tumbles a map, gum wrappers, pens, hair elastics, a half-full water bottle, the stub of my boarding pass, the big fat calculus textbook. Iceman stares at the junk, her eyes narrowing in annoyance.

She kicks the pile. "Her pockets."

Mountain Man pulls the flash drive and the folded brochure from my jacket and hands them to Iceman, who studies them for a brief moment. Her expression tightens. "What did you do with Toby?"

True spies keep their cool under intense pressure. I do nothing of the sort. I blab about how Toby is our friend and how he disappeared and finding the brochure in the jacket in the bathtub.

"Bathtub?" she asks. When I start to explain, she holds up a hand. "Never mind. Here's what I know, *friend* of Toby. He contacted me for help decoding the electronic signature of some wannabe black hat, which I agreed to do for a price. We arranged this meeting. And now no Toby. Instead, you people show up. It's very unprofessional."

My brain races in fast-forward. "Can you still do it?" I ask. "I mean the decoding thing?"

"Thing?" she says, offended. "Of course I can do the decoding 'thing.' Iceman is the *best*."

"She really is," Mountain Man chimes in. "Have you seen her Monster Mayhem level?"

Iceman points at him without looking in his direction. "Go away," she says. "I no longer need you. Tell your friends the operation is over and let the girls go." Mountain Man looks confused. "Do I need to say it again using smaller words?"

"No. Nope. Got it, Boss. All over it." Mountain Man strides away. He's back seconds later, having gone the wrong way out of the maze. Iceman gives an exasperated sigh. "Good people are hard to find," she says. I nod as if I have any idea what she's talking about.

"Now," she says, "my services cost fifty thousand euros."

"Fifty thousand euros?" I blurt.

"That's a deeply discounted rate." She sniffs. "I respect Toby and his work. Even if he is on the wrong side."

"I don't have that kind of money," I say flatly.

"What do you have to offer, then?" she asks, holding me in an icy gaze that goes perfectly with her name.

Think fast, Abby. What can you give instead of money? Nothing. I have nothing. Suddenly, I remember Bad Beret's look of envy while watching Toby. "Bragging rights," I say.

"What?"

"Listen, Toby is world-class, we all know that," I say, hoping she agrees, "so if he needed to buy *your* help, then the black hat behind this hack is really good, right?"

"I follow."

"So if you're better than Toby and you're better than this mysterious black hat, well, that means you're the *best*. You can, uh, put it on your website."

"I don't have a website."

"You know what I mean. Glory."

She eyes me skeptically and finally shrugs. "Perhaps. I'll take a look at what's on the flash drive, but I make no guarantees that I'll do it."

This is better than what I had five minutes ago, which was nothing.

The maze belches us out right into Izumi and Charlotte, who appear annoyed, cold, and very wet. Izumi holds our one umbrella, now mangled beyond recognition. I bet she clobbered someone with it. We do a squishy group hug.

"Guys," I say. "*This* is Iceman. She's going to help us figure out what's on Toby's flash drive."

Izumi gives her a thorough once-over. "No way."

Iceman bristles. "Because I'm not a stupid man, I cannot be a notorious evil mastermind? Why do you assume only men can do this?"

Izumi stares at her feet. He cheeks burn red. "I'm sorry," she mutters. "You're right."

Charlotte throws an arm over Iceman's shoulders. Iceman stiffens.

"This just keeps getting better and better," Charlotte says. "And you're really going to help us?"

"Conditionally help," Iceman corrects.

"Right," I say. "She might help us."

"Can you show us some Monster Mayhem tricks?" asks Charlotte.

"Never," responds Iceman, shrugging off Charlotte. "Come on. Let's get this over with."

Iceman takes us to her apartment in what she calls an unhip *arrondissement* of Paris. Her mother peeks out from the kitchen and gives us a wave. "Bonjour, Izzie. How was your day?"

Izzie?

"Bonjour, Mama," Izzie Iceman replies. "I have some exchange students from school."

"Ah, welcome. Are you girls hungry?"

"Not hungry. We're going to my room."

We travel a long dark hallway and enter the room at the end. Iceman flips on the lights and suddenly we're in a pink explosion. Izumi visibly recoils in horror. Every surface is covered in pink: pink paint, pink bedspread, pink headboard, pink lamps, pink carpet. Along a pink shelf sits a collection of porcelain dolls in pink dresses with pink bows in their hair. There's a mirror in a pink frame with a bunch of photos of pink dresses cut from a magazine taped to it. Even the large computer setup on the pink desk is wrapped in pink tulle. Charlotte's eyes are wide. How does a master hacker named Iceman live in a room like this?

As if reading our minds, she says, "Misdirection. Duh. Oldest trick in the book. A girl like me would never do anything wrong. Works like magic."

"Is your name really Izzie?" asks Charlotte.

Iceman narrows her gaze. "Isabel, to be exact, but you

shall call me Iceman. This is a professional arrangement we're in."

"Sure thing, Izzie," says Charlotte with a wink. Either she's brave or crazy. I don't know which.

The three of us sit on the pink bed and watch as Izzie Iceman hikes up her pink dress and straddles the desk chair. She slides the flash drive in and makes a lot of *ooh* and *aah* sounds that we can't decipher. Does the data mean anything or not? Will she tell us or not? We've probably missed four of Ms. Dunne's phone calls by now. Our punishment will be epic and will last a long time. I put this out of my mind as I watch Iceman's fingers fly over the keyboard. Finally, she leans back in her chair and stretches her arms above her head.

"Have you ever been to Morocco?" she asks. I really want to know what she found, but demanding anything from Iceman seems foolish.

"Once," I say. "With my mother. To Marrakesh."

"That's where I'm from, although I've been in France a long time now." Izzie Iceman seems to drift in thought. "It's easier to get lost in a country like Morocco than it is here, generally speaking. Your hacker's name is Micron. And getting lost is something you might want to consider."

Next to me, Izumi gulps the air.

"Who is this Micron?" Charlotte demands.

"Micron? *Micron?* You don't know who he is?"

"Nope."

"Do you live under a rock?"

"We go to boarding school. Kind of the same thing."

"Micron is responsible for some otherworldly hacks. All those banks that went off-line last year? Micron. Those five days where the airlines couldn't fly because their networks were so screwed up? Micron. That day when all the grades for all the students in California, New York, and Florida vanished forever? Micron. The Hudson River filled with purple bubble bath? Micron. I'm good. Plenty good. Close to the best. But Micron brings it to a whole new level. He's *crazy.*"

She hands me back the flash drive. *This just keeps getting worse.*

"What should we do?" I ask.

"If you're not going to run away and hide, stay out of it," Izzie Iceman says. "You don't want to end up on the wrong side of Micron."

Why do I feel like it's too late for that? All this pink is making me dizzy. I stand abruptly, shoving the flash drive back in my pocket. "Thanks," I say. "We owe you."

"You do," Iceman says. "And one day I will collect."

I don't doubt this at all.

Chapter 15

REAL? NOT REAL.

WE ARRIVE BACK at the Smith School for Children at night. As we pull through the gates, I've never seen two people look as happy as Mr. Lord and Ms. Dunne. They grin ear to ear. They've delivered us back to school, safe and sound. Putting aside the misplacing of Toby and the *Mona Lisa* lockdown, things went pretty well. Our teachers leap out of the school van and vanish immediately, grateful to leave our pack of bedraggled travelers under the watchful eye of someone else, anyone else.

Jennifer welcomes us back in flawless French, commending us on our exemplary behavior. She does not mention *Mona Lisa* at all. I notice dark circles under her eyes. This is extraordinary only because Jennifer Hunter does not get tired. She says she has far too much to do for sleeping. And while she smiles, her jaw is tight.

But no one really listens to her; we fixate on the lock box she carries containing our phones. We might drool, hard to say. As she hands them out, one by one, she reminds us that there's class tomorrow and we should hurry along to our dorms and get some sleep. As if we aren't all going to stay up all night checking in and catching up and watching cat videos. On some things, she is clueless.

In the dorm lobby, we agree to check our idle devices for messages from Toby and search for anything we can find on a hacker called Micron. Having our phones back makes us a little giddy.

"Project Find Toby is on," Izumi says gravely. "Stay in constant contact."

"We share a wall," Charlotte reminds her.

"Well, Abby is *all* the way upstairs."

"I'll sneak down if I find anything," I say. "You guys do the same." We break for our rooms.

We've only been gone a week, but my room smells musty and neglected. My squash uniform is in a heap by the door right where I left it, my racquet chucked in the corner. Sitting on the edge of the unmade bed, I plug in my phone and frantically scroll through all the junk from the last week. Nothing from Toby. I try Find Friends. It says he's off-line. I check his social media feeds. Maybe he posted a photo of himself relaxing on the beach with his dad? But his accounts have been inactive since the day we left for Paris. The disappointment tastes sour in my mouth. Fatigue from a long day settles heavily on my shoulders. *Where* is he?

I text the girls.

Me: *No Toby*

Izumi: *Me either*

Charlotte: *nope*

Me: *move on to Micron*

Izumi: *check back in fifteen minutes*

Fifteen minutes is not very long to crack the identity of a notorious hacker. A search of Micron brings up the Micron Technology company, a specialized kind of Japanese pen, and a million other things unrelated to hacking. My eyelids grow heavy.

Me: *Find anything?*

Silence. My fellow spies have fallen asleep. So much for the urgency of Project Find Toby. I put on my pajamas, climb into bed, and wait for sleep to take me.

It doesn't. Instead, I twitch and roll around like I'm

covered in ants. Despite how tired I am, I can't turn off my brain. It zigs and zags with doomsday scenarios, none of which work out well for Toby. I must fall asleep at some point because I dream that I'm chasing him through thick mist but he remains just out of reach. He yells important things at me in French, and I don't understand. Ms. Dunne would be so disappointed. And then there's an earthquake.

Except it's really Izumi shaking me awake. "Get up already," she says. "We're supposed to be in the headmaster's office in five minutes. And you missed breakfast. You need to get it together, Abby, before you set a world record for demerits."

Tell me about it. I pull on my wrinkled uniform without bothering to brush my hair. So what that it's been three thousand miles and several time zones since its last washing? I throw it up in a ragged ponytail and race after Izumi and Charlotte. Only when we are close do I think to ask what this is about.

"Unknown," says Charlotte. "Best guess is our cover story for Versailles didn't hold."

"No way," I say. "That was some of our best work." After we failed to answer her calls, Ms. Dunne was sure we'd violated the conditions of our agreement. We did a decent enough job acting surprised that our phone wasn't working. But Ms. Dunne is an amateur. Jennifer is a pro.

Right. That. Jennifer waits outside her office. One of her talents is an unreadable face. You can never tell what she's thinking, so it's hard to predict what is in store. A safe bet is nothing good.

"Ladies," Jennifer says. "Have a seat." We squish together on the small couch. Safety in numbers. She takes a seat across from us. We squirm a little under her gaze. "I'm sure you're worried about Toby. I know that you're trying to find him. First, let me say that he's fine. Safe. Healthy. All of that. Second, he may not have been honest with you." That lands with a thud I feel in my stomach muscles. What's she getting at? "He may have concocted a story to get back at his father. He may have led you to believe things that weren't true."

Wait a minute. Is she saying that Toby *fabricated* this whole thing? Impossible. No way. I dig my elbow into Izumi's rib cage.

"Toby and Drexel struggle," Jennifer continues. "I think it just got blown out of proportion this time. But don't worry. Toby will be fine, and he'll be back. I just want you to give him space and privacy in the meantime. Do you understand?"

No! Because Toby wouldn't do that to us. But we nod our

heads because there is no point in arguing with Jennifer. She tells us to hurry to class before we are late.

But how can I concentrate on Chinese History 2 when I am busy fuming at Jennifer? This is a low blow, to suggest that one of my best friends has been lying to me. She must really want to keep me out of this. Hasn't she figured out this sort of misdirection just makes things worse? For a smart person, sometimes my mother is appallingly clueless.

At lunch, we reconvene over dry tuna salad sandwiches and baked potato chips and, really, what's the point of a *baked* potato chip?

"Of course she's lying," I say with a sniff. "I can't believe she'd even try this. Like we're going to believe her? It's crazy."

Charlotte pokes her sandwich with a fork. It barely moves. "It makes a kind of twisted sense," she says quietly.

"Excuse me?"

"Toby really hates Drexel," Izumi adds. "I could see him trying to hurt the thing Drexel loves most. The game."

"Tell me you're kidding." I can't keep the shock off my face. They believe Jennifer's story?

"He could easily have created the messages," Izumi says, "and the fake interface, and he is a total Iceman groupie, so it makes sense that he'd want to meet him. I mean her. I mean Izzie. You know what I mean."

"And Quinn said he's been especially angry lately," says Charlotte. "Like stressed out."

Since when does what Quinn says even matter? But every bit of evidence in support of Toby telling the truth that I toss out, my friends counter with logic. It's incredibly annoying.

"Have you guys talked about this already?" I ask. "You've already made up your minds."

They nod in unison. "We know you don't want it to be true," says Charlotte, "but the more we thought about what Jennifer said, the more sense it made. Toby lied to us."

"But . . ."

"Abby, Project Find Toby is *over.*"

Chapter 16

MONSTER MAYHEM 2.0.

AFTER TWO DAYS, my jet lag is gone, but that doesn't make me feel any better. Charlotte and Izumi act like everything is back to normal, but I just feel hollow. Either one of my best friends was hurting and I totally missed it or he completely lied to me. As options go, they both stink. And what does this say about me? What else am I missing? I'm so distracted that I take a squash ball to the forehead and end up with a black eye. Spying might be dangerous, but self-doubt is worse.

Charlotte sits with me in the infirmary while I hold an ice pack to my face.

"That black and blue will look smashing at Fake Prom," she says with a sly grin.

Fake Prom! That's this weekend! How did I forget? Oh, because I hate it, that's how.

"I might have a concussion," I say. "I can't possibly attend."

"You promised," Charlotte reminds me.

"I might have short-term memory loss."

"Nice try."

"Do I have to?" I whine.

"Yes. For Izumi." She's right. Izumi didn't lie to me. I can't take it out on her.

"Fine," I mutter, shifting the ice. "But no dress."

"Suit yourself," Charlotte says, leaving me alone to freeze my face off.

I slouch in the chair, my head throbbing from the bruise. My friends are smart people, and they seem convinced that Jennifer is right about Toby. I can't discount that I don't want it to be true because if it is, that hurts. What I need is to *ask* Toby. But that's complicated because he's vanished. I can't find a trace of him anywhere. I've taken to carrying my cell phone around in my backpack just in case he makes contact, despite it being against the rules.

It pings merrily now, and I lunge for it, which sends a hot pulse of pain through the back of my skull. Squash is also more dangerous than spying.

It's a text from Jennifer.

Jennifer: *Are you okay?*

Me: *yeah. bump on my head*

Jennifer: *you need to be more careful*

Shouldn't she be telling that to my opponent, Owen Elliott Staar, captain of the varsity boys' team, who had no business playing against me in the first place? Sure, he felt bad about almost knocking me unconscious, but that doesn't mean I have to like him.

Me: *so can I quit squash?*

Jennifer: *No. And why do you have your phone out anyway?*

Boy, you can't win no matter what you do. The Center is always watching.

They *are* always watching! Yes! And I bet one hundred demerits they know where Toby is right now. If I can find him, I can figure out a way to talk to him. I don't need Project Find Toby. I need Project *Talk to* Toby. Why didn't I think of this before?

Well, because it involves breaking into the Catacombs and using the top secret Center communication network.

And I can't get into the Catacombs without the fireplace pass code. That's why.

By the time lights-out rolls around, I've made a decision to sneak into Toby's room. He keeps passwords on random scraps of paper, claiming an unorganized mess is the best security. So it's possible the code is in there. It's also possible it isn't, but let's not worry about that right now. Baby steps.

At midnight, I stand outside Izumi's room, listening for snores. When I'm sure she's asleep, I rummage around in the closet for the tied-together sheets, open the window, and climb out. It's spring, but someone forgot to tell the weather. My breath rises in little puffy clouds. On the ground, every shadow is sinister. I'm jumpy and half convinced this is a very stupid idea.

Lower Middle and Middle boys live in Main Dorm, located on the second floor of Main Hall. I quickly pick the locks to Main Hall and Main Dorm. I've never been in Main Dorm before because girls can't visit boys' rooms, and vice versa, until we're seniors. And even then you have to sign in with the dorm parent and the door must be all the way open. Really, you're better off just hanging out in the Annex.

Dorm rooms don't have locks. We have a "trust, honor,

and respect" policy at Smith. Please note that faculty apartments have dead bolts, and I already told you how trusted we are when it comes to visiting one another's rooms. It should be a "trust, honor, and respect, but only sometimes" policy.

Toby's room is dark, so I flip on my smartphone flashlight. Inside, it's just like mine—a twin bed, a chest of drawers, a desk, a set of bookshelves, and a closet. Bathrooms are locker-room-style at the far end of the hallway. I immediately trip over a shower caddy containing an overturned and oozing shampoo and a dried-out bar of soap. I sweep the light around. Haphazard heaps of clothing clutter the floor, half-detached posters droop with gravity. Books and papers are scattered like snowflakes.

It's a mess. If I didn't know better I'd say this room was recently tossed. Come to think of it, I don't know better. Even though this is my first physical visit to Toby's room, I've been here virtually and I know his desk is end-to-end computers and monitors and gadgets and hard drives. Also, empty Coke cans and candy bar wrappers and a bobblehead from Yankee Stadium. But now it's empty. There's not even a stray cable. His desk drawers are dumped on the floor. I squat down and shift through the contents—pens, markers, tape, torn bits of paper. But nothing with a number sequence similar to the fireplace pass code.

I move to the closet. The only item of clothing still hanging is Toby's wrinkled Smith School blazer. Everything else is in a mound on the floor. The sheets are pulled off his bed and piled in the center of the mattress, which half hangs off the metal bed frame. Someone flipped the mattress and examined underneath it. They were serious, whoever they were.

I go over the room with a fine-tooth comb. I check every inch and every corner. I even look for secret panels in the desk and floor. But all I find is nothing and more nothing. I finish and take a brief pause to despair over the futility of my mission, only to pick back up and examine everything again.

By this point it's late, and my eyes feel like loose marbles rolling around in my head. My bruise aches. I sit down on the crooked mattress before I fall over. This is pointless. It's time to go to bed. I'll think of a new plan tomorrow. My gaze drifts to a note thumbtacked to the bulletin board above Toby's desk. It says, in big capital letters, TOBY IS COOL. "Toby is cool" was the pass code for my old spy phone, and I had to say it every time I wanted to enter a command. It was really annoying.

"Ha," I say under my breath. "Toby is cool. That's a joke.

If Toby was really cool, he'd have texted me or something. That's what friends do."

From the dark recesses of the closet comes the quietest little beep. It's so quiet I almost think I imagined it. "Toby is cool," I whisper again into the dark room. *BEEP*. I crawl into the closet, pushing the clothes aside and whispering, "Toby is cool," like a demented mantra.

The beep comes from above my head, from the inside pocket of the hanging blazer. I yank it down and give it a shake over the mattress. Out falls a slim smartphone, clad in a pink plastic case with the name ABBY spelled out in tiny rhinestones. Rhinestones? Who is he kidding with the rhinestones? The screen glows intermittently, winking at me.

"Toby is cool," I say, loud as I dare.

Beep! The screen lights up with a smiley face and a big WELCOME! This morphs into fireworks and balloons. I'm barely breathing. "Phone open."

A burst of color floods the screen, and several app icons float into view. If my phone was 1.0, this has to be somewhere in the threes. It's way fancy. Why didn't Toby tell me about it? Oh, I forgot. Toby doesn't tell me anything. The apps drift around the small screen like jellyfish trailing iridescent tendrils. Only when the apps settle down do I get a look at them. Some are familiar: hot water spray, rubber bullets, and screaming sirens. And others are new. A lightning bolt, a ninja throwing star, a sword. *Oh, wow. A sword?* But before I can tap any of them, shuffling footsteps in the hallway grab my attention. I crack the door just enough to see who's out there. Tucker! Wearing saggy pajama bottoms, he yawns and scratches his armpit on his way toward the bathroom. About halfway there, he stops to pick something off the sole of his foot. This is my chance. I get down low, aim the glitzy phone, and whisper, "Toby is cool. Lightning bolt."

The phone grows warm in my hand. A split second later, the hallway fills with a blinding, pulsing light. I pitch forward on my knees. Tucker howls with confusion. The light thumps like a heart, like a disco ball inserted directly into my brain. Toby's lightning bolt creates complete and total disorientation. I open half an eye to see Tucker staggering around the hallway, one hand holding up his pajama pants, the other outstretched in front of him. He bumps square into the wall, bounces off, and lands on his butt.

"Webster?" he growls. "Is that you?" Webster Franks is a small kid in my grade who often spends time in the Cavanaugh Family Meditative Pond and Fountain, compliments of Tucker. I think about Webster paddling around in the muddy water, soggy school blazer dragging him down and glasses askew while Tucker's posse stands on dry land and laughs.

It would be kind of cool for Tucker to be a little afraid of Webster, right? Score one for the invisibles? As the pulsating light begins to fade, I tap the app again.

"Stop!" Tucker cries. "I'm begging you! I can't take it!" He squashes his palms into his eye sockets, but that doesn't help. Toby's disorientation lightning bolt is experienced from the inside out. And I know what Toby would say about it. It will buy you some time. I miss Toby.

Tucker hauls himself to his feet and lurches down the hallway toward the bathroom. He moves like a zombie. When he crashes through the bathroom door, I hear a splash. It's possible he just fell in the toilet.

I should have taken video. No one is going to believe me.

When I'm sure Tucker is not going to suddenly grow brave and come back to investigate, I dash for the stairs. Safely back in my room, I examine the phone more closely. The rhinestones aren't an upgrade, but the rest of it is. So while I'm overjoyed, I'm also back to square one. The sparkly Abby phone does not have the Center communications app, and I don't have a pass code for the fireplace.

But just as my finger hovers above the sword app

(because of course now I have to!), a familiar sound rings out. *TADA!*

What? I quickly swipe to the second page of apps. And there it is. Monster Mayhem 2.0. When I open it, bright colors fill the screen, swirling like wind funnels.

WELCOME, TOBY!

A fuzzy purple monster with fangs pops up and gives me a casual wave. I'm logged in to Toby's account! He must have put Monster Mayhem 2.0 on my new phone and tested it using his own credentials. He just forgot to log out. Within seconds, I determine that Toby is near Washington, DC, and he just caught a Snallygaster, a nasty dragonlike creature who supposedly hangs out in those parts. The Snallygaster is hard-core platinum. Toby also caught a Goatman near Baltimore.

My heart races. Toby isn't tucked away having quality time with Drexel. He didn't try to mess up Monster Mayhem to get back at him. No way. Toby is *playing* Micron's game.

Everything he told us is *true.*

Chapter 17

CAT GOT YOUR TONGUE?

I STAY UP MUCH TOO LATE, being mad at Jennifer and mad at Charlotte and Izumi and mad at myself for doubting Toby and mad at Toby for not telling us anything. I feel betrayed. And because being mad and betrayed is exhausting, I sleep through breakfast and school meeting, which means I can't tell the girls they are wrong until lunchtime. Of course, my plans go sideways the minute they see the rhinestones.

"Where did you get that, and what are *those*?" Charlotte asks.

"Rhinestones," I say. "Never mind. Listen. Toby is *playing.*"

"Rhinestones?" Izumi says with a grin. "For real?"

"Stop it," I command. "Pay attention."

"Okay. Okay. Relax," Charlotte responds. "Nothing wrong with a little glitter." They crack up. I've lost them.

"Toby's telling the truth about the game," I say flatly. "And I have proof." This gets their attention. I fill in the details. I lose them again briefly when I get to the part about the lightning bolt.

"You did *not*."

"Yeah. He fell in the toilet." This gets me high fives all around. When I finish the story, Charlotte furrows her eyebrows.

"Why should we care?" she asks. "He left us in the *Mona Lisa* room. He didn't tell us *anything*."

"Exactly," adds Izumi. "He's on his own. And I think that's the way he likes it. Let me see that thing." She swipes the phone, zooming in on Toby's activity and studying his last captures. "Hey, you guys," she says finally. "Look at this!" She points to what is supposed to be Toby's next capture, a Skunk Ape in Florida.

"What's a Skunk Ape?" asks Charlotte. "Sounds gross. How come all these creatures are gross? Where are the cute ones?"

"A Skunk Ape is the Southern version of a bigfoot," I

say. "It smells like a rotting corpse from sleeping in alligator dens."

"It's a little weird you keep knowing these things," Charlotte responds.

"This is a problem." Izumi uses her fingers to manipulate the background map. "A big problem."

"What?" Charlotte demands.

"It's southern Florida," Izumi hisses. "The *spy college* is also in southern Florida." She zooms in even more. The edges of the Florida Keys come into view along with a platinum cage, indicating the general location of the Skunk Ape.

"We don't even know where the spy college is," I remind her.

"You guys don't pay attention. Did you even see the background when Jennifer was talking to Veronica? The Blue Diamond Hotel sign?"

There was something other than palm trees? The screen is now tight in on a building identified as the Blue Diamond Hotel on Key West.

"So the spy college is in Key West?" I ask.

Izumi rolls her eyes. "Of course not. It's on Fleming Key." Her tone implies we ought to know why this is so obvious. Her face reflects disappointment at our cluelessness. "Ugh. Come on. Fleming Key is military, off-limits to civilians. The cage is right over Fleming Key. Veronica took Jennifer's call from the beach. She must have been on the move. Micron obviously wants Toby to break into the spy college and catch the Skunk Ape. It's madness. No one can do that. If he gets caught, he's finished."

"The *Mona Lisa* was bad enough," Charlotte says, shoving a slice of apple into her mouth and chomping it to bits. "There's no way Toby can get in and out of the spy college undetected."

"And if they catch him in there, they'll accuse him of treason," adds Izumi.

Well, when you put it that way . . .

"I'm going to Florida," I announce. I can't just leave him to his fate, no matter how mad I am at him.

"You are not," replies Izumi.

"I didn't say you had to come with me," I shoot back.

"I guess breaking into a secret military facility and capturing a stinky bigfoot might be fun," Charlotte says. *Yes! Charlotte is in!*

"We're *not* breaking in," I insist. "We're going to stop Toby from breaking in. It's different."

"Why don't you just call him?" Izumi asks.

"You think I didn't already try that?" This phone can do many things, but contacting Toby is not one of them.

"How would we even get to Florida? Magic carpet? Broomstick? How is Toby getting to Florida?"

"Slowly," I say. "Walking. Hitchhiking. Maybe the bus? He had to catch a Snallygaster and a Goatman. That couldn't have been easy. And it looks like he takes a lot of detours to catch regular creatures because his health keeps going yellow." His erratic path is probably why no one has caught him yet.

"Just so we're clear," says Izumi. "You think we should *walk* to Florida? Do you know how long that will take?"

"I didn't say that! And I don't know!"

We go back and forth like this for a bit until Charlotte holds up her hands. "Wait. I have an idea. Izumi, quick, how many more days will it take Toby to walk to spy college? Best estimate."

Izumi studies Toby's Monster Mayhem trail, closes her eyes for a second, and says, "Seventy-six hours and forty-two minutes. Give or take."

"Three days. Fake Prom is in three days."

"So what?"

"Well, we don't have to check in or out of anything from the end of classes Friday until Sunday dinner."

She's right about that. There are no sports on Fake

Prom Saturday, no attendance at dinner, and no breakfast requirement. The school is banking on students not running away to Florida during this time.

"All we have to do is get to the airport and I can arrange for KC's jet to take us to Florida." (For the record, KC is Kingston Cavendish, Charlotte's father.) "We stop Toby and are back before anyone knows we're gone!"

I like Charlotte's plan, but jets are kind of big. "You're saying KC won't notice that his plane is missing?"

"He's in Berlin," Charlotte says. "Besides, he only notices me when I'm standing right in front of him and then only maybe."

"Won't the pilots just refuse?" I ask.

Charlotte sighs. "Do you guys have so little faith in me? I can get the pilots to take me *anywhere*."

"No," I say. "We totally believe you." I'm sure she could convince them to try for Mars, given the chance.

Izumi stares at us. "You're not serious. You can't be serious. This is the most ridiculous, doomed-to-spectacular-failure plan you've ever hatched. I won't let you do it."

At the end of a heated discussion, during which Izumi begrudgingly accepts her fate, we agree we'll act normally until Saturday afternoon. We will then leave campus and steal a plane. Charlotte insists it's not stealing because the plane belongs to her father, who is not using it at the moment, and aren't we all taught in kindergarten to share, so what's the big deal? Izumi and I agree that if Charlotte doesn't see it as a big deal there is no way for us to explain it to her.

Before we can clear our trays, we're interrupted by a noisy herd of sophomore boys. They descend on our table like locusts. Their overflowing food trays clatter as they fill the empty seats. These are the lacrosse boys, the football boys, the ice hockey boys. They do not sit with Middles. More specifically, they do not sit with us. Parker Ramirez is among them, grinning slyly, like he has just the best secret. Izumi flushes.

"What do you want?" Charlotte asks.

"We're almost done," I add. "You can have the table."

"Nice black eye!" says Owen Elliott Staar, Parker's BFF and the one responsible for the black eye in the first place.

"I don't think you're supposed to admire your work," I snap.

"The problem is you plant your feet," he says in all seriousness, "when you need to be ready to move. If you bounce a little, the ball never catches you off guard." Is he really critiquing my squash performance? Parker elbows him before he can move on to what is wrong with my serve. He clears his throat and smiles too widely. We don't fear this crew like we do Tucker. But even with Parker's reputation for being a nice guy, I'm nervous. There's something unnatural at work here.

"Anyway, we're here to talk to you guys," Owen Elliott says. "Well, not exactly you guys." He points at Izumi. "Her."

"Me?"

"Yup."

I'm filled with sudden dread. Did Parker find out Izumi likes him? Is this some sort of ritual humiliation to put her in her place? I have the bedazzled iPhone tucked in my jacket pocket, and I'm ready to draw the sword even if I have no idea what will happen when I do. I can't let these boys be mean to Izumi. Charlotte shoots me an alarmed look.

"Parker's got something he'd like to ask you," Owen Elliott says. The other boys at the table nod and grunt and throw out some "yeah"s and "do it, man"s. I hold my breath. Izumi loses her rosy glow and swings toward deadly pale. The rest of the dining hall has gone silent, all eyes on us. "Okay, Parker. You're on, friend."

Is Parker blushing? Why, yes he is. He's also stammering, stuttering, wringing his hands, and holding his breath.

"Hey, wait a minute," Charlotte blurts out. "Are you asking Izumi to Fake Prom? Is that what's going on here?"

Parker exhales in a rush. "Yes! Thank you! I'm dying here! Will you go with me, Izumi?"

"Nothing like waiting until the last minute to make a person feel special," Charlotte says, indignant. But Izumi's eyes sparkle. She looks only at Parker and he at her. I half expect little hearts to start swirling around their heads. This is great and all, I get that, but what about Florida? And Project Rescue Toby Before He Commits Treason?

I'm about to nudge Izumi, to remind her of our Saturday escape plans, when Charlotte punches me in the thigh. "If you open your mouth and ruin this for her, I'll kill you," she whispers.

"So what do you say, Sato, will you go with me?" He calls her by her last name. How romantic. Charlotte makes fake gagging sounds. I punch *her* in the thigh. Izumi looks at Charlotte and me as if for permission. Charlotte nods encouragingly. I don't and get punched again.

"Yes," Izumi says, so quietly Parker asks her to repeat her answer for clarification. Owen Elliott claps his hands and the other boys whoop and holler. And just as suddenly as they arrived, they leave. They don't even say good-bye.

Boys are weird.

The show over, the rest of the dining hall turns back to the business of lunch. The mean-girl table glares in our direction, but that's to be expected. Parker is not a senior, but he is clearly one of theirs and they are not happy.

Izumi is dazed. I snap my fingers in front of her face a few times. "Hey," I say. "Are you okay?"

"Did that just happen?" she asks.

"Yes," Charlotte confirms. "In front of the whole world."

Izumi leaps from the table, upsetting her glass of cranberry juice. "What am I going to wear?" she yells.

"Sit," Charlotte says, yanking her back down. Izumi buries her head in her hands. She's sweating and a funny shade of green.

"I can't do this," she says, hyperventilating.

"Why not?" I ask. "It's a stupid dance."

"With *Parker*?"

"It's what you wanted," I remind her.

"Yes, I wanted it, but did I *really* want it?"

"Calm down," Charlotte says, stroking Izumi's hair like she's a cat. "Deep breaths. We'll be right there with you. Won't we, Abby?"

No, we won't. We'll be on a stolen plane en route to Florida. My friends eyeball me, waiting. Am I supposed to surrender to Fake Prom? Forget it. I'm going to Florida.

"*Right*, Abby?" Charlotte says again. Izumi looks happier in this moment than I've ever seen her. The permanent crease between her eyebrows is temporarily gone.

"Of course," I say. "I mean, I'm not dressing up or anything or going with a date, but I'll be there. Sure."

"I think I'm going to throw up," Izumi says. She runs from the table like she's not kidding. Charlotte leaves next, saying she might as well accept some senior named Grant's invitation to go with him. Didn't she just bash Parker for waiting until the last minute?

Girls are weird too.

I sit alone at the table with my kale-and-white-bean paste sandwich and think about how much grief I'd get if I just cried for a while. There aren't many people left in the dining hall, but the headmaster's daughter sobbing into her leftovers would surely ignite the gossip fire. Probably it would end up as a video on YouTube before dinner.

But I do want to just . . . cry. Five minutes ago we were contemplating the best Smith School escape in the history of the world, and now the talk is all useless Fake Prom and dates and dresses. Where's the adventure in that? How did my friends become so sidetracked so fast? And how did I end up the odd girl out?

Chapter 18

ALIENS HAVE ABDUCTED MY FRIENDS. I SHOULD CALL SOMEONE.

I JUST DON'T GET IT. This date with Parker has completely rewired Izumi's brain in less than twenty-four hours. And Charlotte is happily caught up in the madness. My friends dig through two large steamer trunks full of curated party dresses, sent compliments of Charlotte's mother, while I lie on Charlotte's bed and stare at the ceiling. There is enough lace and taffeta and tulle and sequins in here to suffocate a pageant queen. I'm not surprised at Charlotte's delight in trying on dresses because this is normal for her. But Izumi is terrifying. She squeals at each new treasure pulled from the trunks, red-faced and so excited I can see her heart pounding through her Smith

School T-shirt. Charlotte keeps throwing dresses at me, but I plan on being on a bus to Florida, and that doesn't require a party dress.

I try to bring the conversation back around to something meaningful: the fact that Toby is slowly making his way south toward his date with certain doom. But competing with taffeta and silk and lace for my friends' attention is not easy. They have been replaced by bizarre alien girlie girls.

"Do you like this one?" Charlotte asks. She spins around in a beaded red dress.

"You won't be able to breathe," I point out.

"It's *amazing*," says Izumi. "But I also love the blue one on you."

There's more squealing and commentary on fabric and cut, and eventually I can't take it and drift out of Charlotte's room.

It's twenty minutes until lights-out, and I decide to walk over to the Annex and buy cheese fries because sometimes that's all a girl can do. It's a cold, clear night and the stars are crisp in the sky. I circle around the Cavanaugh Meditative Pond and Fountain and throw open a set of French doors leading to the Annex. It's crowded and hot and buzzing with talk of Fake Prom. This does not make me feel better.

Cheese fries in hand, I sit alone and watch my fellow students laughing and smiling until the warning bell for lights-out blasts me from my seat. But instead of heading back to McKinsey House, I drift past the senior girls' dorm, across the footbridge spanning Crooked Creek, around a Lower School soccer field, and right to the front door of the headmaster's residence.

The residence sits atop a small hill, with a view of the expansive Smith campus. It's a classic New England house with a cedar shingle roof, black shutters, and white siding. A brick pathway leads to the heavily lacquered black front door from which a brass rhinoceros head knocker hangs. There are easily a dozen windows along the front side of the house, all dark but for one.

I skip the brass rhino and rap gently with my knuckles. After a moment, the door swings open and there is Jennifer. She's shed her headmaster uniform of khaki suit, white shirt, and high heels for sweatpants and a Smith hoodie.

"You don't have to knock," she says. "This is your house too." But we both know it isn't. I've never spent a night in this place. She hugs me as I brace for the *what are you doing here, it's lights-out in two minutes?* speech. But instead she calls the McKinsey House dorm mother and tells her I'll be late.

The house is furnished with heavy brocades, velvet drapes, and furniture named after English kings. There's not a single thing here that was in our apartment. An alarming thought hits me. If Mrs. Smith doesn't come back as headmaster soon, I could be facing a summer in this house. I shudder at the thought. *Who will I hang out with? Faculty kids? Cows?*

Before I can get too depressed over a summer in the country, Jennifer steers me into the cavernous kitchen. No wonky puke-green oven here. Everything is stainless steel, shiny, and new. I sit at the large farmer's table while Jennifer sticks a mug of water in the microwave for hot cocoa. I'll bet a hundred dollars Jennifer has never turned on any appliance in this kitchen other than the microwave.

As she slides the mug in front of me, she says, "What's up?"

I want to tell her about how strange my friends are acting and how our quest to save Toby from himself was so quickly supplanted by boys and dresses. I want to tell her about how bad I am at squash, how I have so many demerits I've lost count, and how everything I want to do, everything that feels natural to me, is wrong. I've had all these experiences since coming to Smith, but at the end of the day I'm still the kid sitting in the principal's office while he tells her mother about the most recent "bad choices." I don't want to be that person.

But I can't say any of that. Instead, I say, "Nothing."

"Are you going to Spring Fling?" she asks casually. "I hear Izumi and Charlotte are."

"They're acting so weird," I blurt.

Jennifer sits down across from me. Her long blond hair is in a bun held in place by a pencil, and her violet eyes are sharp. "How are they weird?"

"The stupid dance! They're suddenly obsessed with dresses."

"Sometimes our friends act strangely," she says. "It's important to remember that they're just people with moods and stresses and things that bother them. We have to treat them like we'd want to be treated when things feel a little off. They're excited by something that doesn't excite you. Try and be glad for them. It doesn't mean you have to share their enthusiasm for stupid dances and dresses, but don't hold it against them."

I hate it when she's right.

Jennifer slides a mug of hot cocoa in front of me. "Listen. When our friends are struggling or testing out something new, that's when they need us most. That's when we need to set aside our own feelings, just for a bit. Do you know what I mean?"

A warm glow rises in my chest, and it's not from the hot drink. Did she just say that when our friends are in trouble, that's when they need us the most? I'm certain she did. But I double-check anyway.

"What you're saying is that when our friends are in trouble, we should do something?"

She raises a perfect eyebrow at me and says, "I *said* when our friends are experimenting with different versions of themselves, we should be patient and tolerant. Don't twist my words."

I'm not twisting. I'm interpreting. And in my interpretation, she's practically begging me to rescue Toby before he does something really stupid.

Jennifer asks if I want to stay overnight in the residence, but I tell her I'm happy in my ugly fourth-floor dorm room. This is not a total lie. I have made peace with my room, but I also need my computer to figure out the best way to get to Florida before Toby does. And it can't be walking.

As Jennifer escorts me back to my dorm, she goes on and on about exciting new changes to the dining hall menu. I stop listening when she brings up edamame hummus. She lets me into McKinsey House, gives me a kiss on the head, and tells me to go straight to bed. Naturally, I don't.

Instead, I fire up my laptop and search bus routes to Florida. Thirty-eight hours and forty-five minutes! And that's the *fast* route. A person could evolve into another species in that amount of time. I turn my attention to plane tickets. This would be easier if I weren't under eighteen. You can't do anything in this country if you're under eighteen, except get bossed around by people who are *over* eighteen. It's not fair. If I want to go to Florida to rescue my friend, who might accidentally commit treason, that should be my right. Why do I have to ask permission? The airline website doesn't care about this injustice. It just wants me to fly with a parent or have permission from one.

I sit back and consider my options. Maybe if I show up at the airport, pay cash, and fly standby they won't notice I'm too young? Jennifer and I have done that a number of times, and she always gets on. Probably that's because national security is on the line and someone has made a phone call saying she'd better get a seat or else. But what are the chances of me getting away with it? I'll tell you. Zero. I'm sure I'm on every no-fly list, not because I've done anything bad (or really bad anyway) but because Jennifer knows how to make things happen. Her book of tradecraft tricks must be as thick as the Manhattan phone book that no one uses anymore. More likely, all that information is tucked away in her head. And yet here she is running the Smith School while the real headmaster gets sorted out.

She must be so bored. Is it like a Beginning Concepts in Physics class that never ends? Is my running away to Florida just going to make it worse?

A message from Izumi pops up on my laptop.

Izumi: *where did you go?*

Me: *to see Jennifer*

Izumi: *are you ok?*

Me: *yes*

Izumi: *I'm sorry about the dresses and stuff*

My throat goes tight. I remember what Jennifer said about being happy for my friends even if I'm not happy for myself. I figure I'll give it a go.

Me: *don't be! I like the purple dress, btw. Looks good on you. Parker will drool!*

Izumi: *he's just a big dumb football player*

Me: *he likes you*

Izumi: *excuse me. I might have to throw up again.*

The screen goes dark. Maybe she really did have to throw up? I can't imagine ever feeling that way over a boy. Sometimes I've been so scared I want to puke, but that seems like a reasonable human reaction if your life is in jeopardy. I wait to see if she returns, but she doesn't.

I *am* happy for Izumi. She's so smart it's intimidating. And some kids call her snooty when really she's just shy. But at her core, she's fiery, which is obvious if you watch her rugby games. She will show no mercy in pursuit of the win. In those situations, it's best to just get out of the way. And she's loyal. No *way* Parker is good enough for her. I don't care how nice he is.

I sit back. The first thing I need to accept is I will be riding the bus. There is no way to sneak onto a plane, and no one appears to care how old you are if you're running away by bus. Being a spy sometimes calls for discomfort. The four-hundred-hour bus ride will be a character-building exercise. I just hope I get there before Toby does.

The second thing is I will be going alone. This creates a pit of sadness in my stomach that I don't want to deal with, so I put my head on my pillow and close my eyes against it.

Chapter 19

AND SOMETIMES YOU GET SURPRISED.

AS IS TRADITION, the Friday of Spring Fling weekend is declared a "free day" by Headmaster Hunter. A free day means that classes are canceled and the students have no obligations. They can wear pajamas and hang out in the Annex eating cheese fries all day. But most of us make a pilgrimage to downtown Watertown. For normal kids, walking downtown is no big deal, but for prisoners of the Smith School it's an event.

We skirt along the bordering stonewall for about ten minutes, puddles from the rain soaking our shoes, before a cut-through lands us on the sidewalk. I've been roped into wearing a dark blue, alarmingly sparkly confection to

Spring Fling that my best friends say makes me look fabulous. But I know better. I look ridiculous, like a little kid who fell in the dress-up box. They refused my plea to wear regular clothes. I have no date. My job is to stand around in case Izumi needs me. Couldn't I do that in track pants? But I guess it doesn't matter because I will only be wearing the dress for a little while. On Saturday night, at seven o'clock sharp, my plan is to sneak away, ditch the dress, and get to the bus stop. If my calculations are correct, and let's hope they are, I should arrive almost exactly when Toby does.

Spontaneous little rivers run down the long hill to the main drag of downtown. Main Street Watertown was probably cute when horses and carriages were cutting-edge technology, but now it leans toward run-down. There are several shuttered storefronts, dusty FOR SALE signs hanging in their doors. There's a pharmacy, a convenience store, a used bookstore, and Sweetness Reigns, a candy shop with wall-to-wall bins of sugary goodness. Fill a paper bag for a flat rate of ten dollars. It might be the best thing about boarding school. I assume this is our destination because whenever we get a chance to break for downtown, Sweetness Reigns is where we end up.

But today Charlotte drags us into the used bookstore. "We have to make a stop." A small bell over the door announces our arrival. Dust floats in the light thrown off from a dangling bulb.

"Hello?" Charlotte yells. Her voice is immediately absorbed by hundreds of tattered books. Warped shelves fill every available space. The proprietor surely likes to buy used books, but does she ever sell any? A woman with long gray braids emerges from a back room hidden by a cascade of beads. She wears thick black-framed glasses that give her giant bug eyes. Her lips are a slash of bright red.

"Ah, Charlotte." She coughs a few times to clear her throat. "Sorry. Sorry. I just got a collection from one of the old estates up on Maple, and I'm sure there are mold spores in there."

Mold spores. Wonderful. Charlotte gives the woman a big hug, as if they are long-lost friends. I should point out that Charlotte has never mentioned the bookstore woman before. I try to catch Izumi's eye, but she watches Charlotte.

"So we're set for tomorrow, then?" Charlotte asks with an unfamiliar lilt. Charlotte has a lot of voices. She uses them like disarming spells. I mentally catalog this new one as "old-lady bookstore voice."

"Yes," the lady says. "Eight thirty, in the parking lot across from the main gates. Headlights off, inconspicuous and all that."

"Yes. Perfect," says Charlotte. The lady holds out her hand expectantly, and Charlotte fills it with an envelope from inside her parka. The corner of the envelope lifts, exposing the sharp edges of crisp new bills.

"What's going on?" I whisper. Izumi elbows me and holds a finger to her lips. Clearly, I'm the only one not in the know. Charlotte hugs the lady again and hustles us back out onto the sidewalk, where I plant my feet and refuse to move until an explanation is offered.

"Relax," Charlotte says with a wink. "Just lining things up for tomorrow night."

"What do you mean?"

"Florida, idiot," Izumi says, punching me in the shoulder.

"But . . . ," I sputter. They aren't coming with me. They're going to Fake Prom with dates and fancy dresses and shoes that give them blisters. I'm going on the bus alone. "You're coming with me?"

"You didn't think we'd let you have all the fun, did you?" Charlotte asks.

"Well, I just thought that . . . What about Parker and Grant?"

Izumi rolls her eyes dramatically. "Boys. Whatever." I give them a fierce hug. I hug so hard Charlotte grunts.

"You guys are amazing," I say, a lump in my throat.

"We totally *know* that," Charlotte responds.

We head down the street toward Sweetness Reigns. "So where is Bookstore Lady taking us in the inconspicuous car?" I ask.

"To the airport. The plane is ready to go."

"Seriously?"

"Yup."

"You actually did it?"

"You doubted me?"

"No. Never. Not at all."

Izumi laughs. "All three of us rolled together make one seriously good spy."

She's right. Our skills are complementary. We make a brilliant package.

We meet everyone we know in Sweetness Reigns. Izumi and Parker bump into each other by the gummy bears.

"Hi," he mumbles. The signs say DO NOT SAMPLE THE CANDY, but Parker's mouth is full of multicolored SweeTARTS.

Izumi freezes. Charlotte nudges her with an elbow. "Hi," Izumi blurts. "Funny that you're here and I'm here and we're both here in, you know, this store."

Oh, boy. This could get awkward. Parker's posse circles,

concerned looks on their faces. What do they think Izumi is going to? Bury Parker in candy corn? Steal his chocolate-covered raisins? No, the big gossips, they just want to hear what happens.

"Yeah, it is funny," says Parker, his cheeks coloring. "Do you, um, like cinnamon bears?"

Owen Elliott Staar face-palms his forehead. Charlotte cringes. Izumi and Parker are the very definition of uncool.

"I do," replies Izumi, with great seriousness. "They're the best."

"I'm really excited about tomorrow night," Parker says softly.

"Me too! Me too. I mean, I am also."

I lean over to Charlotte and whisper, "Please end this."

She nods. "Agreed. It's like they have both lost their minds. Izumi!" Izumi glances at us as if in a daze. "We have to go. Now."

We each grab an arm and drag her out of the store. How are we ever going to get her away from Parker tomorrow night? *Tomorrow night.* My chest goes tight with gratitude and anticipation. I can't imagine how Charlotte finally talked Izumi into this caper, our most outrageous by far. I mean, we're stealing a *plane*. That elevates things to a certain level, doesn't it? And while Charlotte and I seem comfortable breaking the rules, Izumi does not. Plus, she is so obviously excited about Fake Prom with Parker. But I underestimate Charlotte's powers of persuasion at my own peril. Whatever happens, I don't have to go to Florida alone.

Last year, the idea of doing something stupid by myself would have been fine. In fact, I preferred it. Less drama, less negotiation, less managing of other people's feelings. But last night, when I thought I was on my own, I felt nothing but sadness. I hope they know how much this means to me, even if I'm lousy at showing it.

And I hope they forgive me when we get kicked out of school for going AWOL.

Chapter 20

RHINESTONES AND A PINK CADILLAC.

CHARLOTTE IS BUSY painting my lips with tinted lip balm while I try and ask her how much money she put in that envelope.

"Shhhh!" she scolds. "You're messing up my work!"

"It was four hundred dollars," Izumi says.

"Four *hundred* dollars? Where did you get four hundred dollars?" The lip balm slides up and bumps my nose.

Charlotte exhales, exasperated. "KC gives me cash whenever we see each other."

"Doesn't he know you can't use it on campus?"

"Doesn't know. Doesn't care. But that seemed a fair price for transport out of here under the cloak of darkness."

Izumi runs the brush one more time through her long black hair. "So?" She spins. Her purple dress fits perfectly, the color highlighting her rosy cheeks.

"You look really beautiful," I say. "Parker's going to freak." This makes her squeal and jump up and down. I may never get used to this.

Another way Fake Prom isn't like a real prom is that students meet their dates in the decked-out dining hall, done up this year with glitter-encrusted giant glowing sunflowers and twinkly lights. It looks like a craft store blew up in here. Charlotte twirls off in Grant's direction. Parker waits for Izumi by the double doors. He wears an ill-fitting suit and flip-flops. His face is shiny and hopeful and he offers Izumi a shy smile. His posse stands back about four feet and fist-bumps and high-fives, like a demented Greek chorus.

"Hey, Hunter!" yells Owen Elliott. "Where's your date?"

"I threw him in the pond," I say flatly. Owen Elliott approaches, putting his hand up for a high five. I study my cuticles.

"Whatever," he says, running his fingers through his spiky brown hair. "I thought you railroaded Toby into taking you."

"No." *Toby is missing, in case you haven't noticed.*

"Well, gotta get in there and make some noise. Have fun, Hunter. No more black eyes, okay? Don't plant those feet!" He laughs as he saunters off, and I find myself standing all alone outside the dining hall wishing Toby were here to stand all alone with me.

I check my watch. Charlotte said my battered old Timex did not go with the blue sequins, but I don't care. I want to know exactly how many minutes I have to endure this nightmare before we make our escape. Izumi calculated that if we leave at 8:47, we will arrive at Spy College right before Toby. So only thirty-seven minutes and forty-two seconds to go. An eternity. I take a deep breath and enter the dining hall.

Only to bump directly into Ms. Dunne and Mr. Lord. They look weird all dressed up, especially Mr. Lord, who wears a threadbare tuxedo with pants that are four inches too short and reveal mismatched argyle socks.

"Abby!" Suddenly, Jennifer appears between them.

Oh, no. I can't be anywhere near Jennifer. She will sniff the air and just *know* I'm up to something. It is mission critical I get away from her ASAP. "Don't you look nice?"

Is this a rhetorical question? Do I usually answer them? What's normal?

"Thanks!" I smile brightly. Probably too brightly. I'm going to get us busted before we even get a chance to do anything wrong.

"I'm glad you came," she says with a wink.

"Are you having fun?" asks Ms. Dunne. No. Fun would be pizza back in the dorm lounge in my track pants. This is not fun. This is torture. A bead of sweat runs down my back. The pink iPhone, tucked up under my dress, vibrates. I jump. Jennifer narrows her gaze.

"Are you okay?" she asks. Must. Escape. Now.

"I hear there's sushi!" I blurt.

"It's to die for," says Mr. Lord. He squeezes Jennifer's arm as if he might swoon from the very idea of a sushi bar. Jennifer gives his hand a *look*, the kind that says *why are you touching me?* The phone buzzes continually now. A good spy recognizes a chance for escape and takes it.

"I'm off to check it out!" I don't even like sushi. I hope this is something Jennifer does not remember about me. I cut around Owen Elliott Staar, who, true to his word, is making a lot of noise, and beeline to the bathrooms at the back of the dining hall. They, too, are decorated with sunflowers and twinkly lights. I bump a flower as I dash into the stall farthest from the door. Glitter sticks to my forehead. With some effort I roll my dress up my thighs until the phone falls out. I catch it midair and take a seat on the closed toilet.

Toby is getting close to his destination. The buzz is a warning that his health is critically low. I click the phone off because augmented reality games are a real battery drain. I slide it back up my dress, where it makes a hot rectangle against my thigh. When my watch hits 8:40, I grin like an idiot. Our Fake Prom is officially over.

I spot Izumi first, slow dancing with Parker at the very center of the dining hall dance floor. For two athletes, they are stiff and awkward, holding each other at a distance and grinning like idiots. How do I do this gracefully?

Who cares? I have no time for graceful. I tap Izumi on the shoulder.

"Um. Excuse me. Sorry."

Parker's big grin falters. "What do you want?"

"I need to talk to Izumi."

"Now?"

Why does this big dope think I need his permission to speak to my friend? He's a little bit possessive for my taste. Izumi puts herself between us before things get worse. "It's fine. It will just take a minute."

"Fine," says Parker. "You can cut in, but only for this dance. Okay, Hunter?"

"Yes, sir," I say, giving him a mock salute. I step into his position and put my arms around Izumi. I lean in close and whisper, "It's time to go," in her ear because Parker remains standing, hands in pockets, about ten inches from us. Immediately, conflict clouds her face, and guilt overwhelms me. "Maybe you should stay," I offer.

Izumi steels herself. "No. No, I'm in. Where's Charlotte?"

"I don't know. I have to find her."

"Okay. Let's meet outside the Main Hall doors in ten minutes." Her eyes drift longingly back to Parker, and I step aside. He slides right into my spot, once again wearing the big grin, and I wonder how Izumi is going to get away from him short of beating him up.

I begin my search for Charlotte on the dance floor. She's not there. I search the area where the food is set up. Not there, either. I finally find her siting on the steps of the junior boys' dorm entertaining about ten of them with a story about how she got avalanched in Switzerland and was rescued by a handsome Frenchman named Sebastian and his dog Claude. Her telling is very dramatic. She leaves out the bit about how the snow really only covered her up to her ankles. The boys are rapt. They can't take their eyes off her. I can almost see Charlotte's magic pixie dust glinting in the light.

When she sees me, she says, "Okay, boys. Story time is over. Go away. I'm busy." Like dutiful minions, they scatter, with murmured "thank you"s and urgent "see you later?"s. I'll admit I'm surprised to see Izumi outside the Main Hall doors, shivering with the cold. I was worried Parker might have locked her in a closet or something.

We stay in the shadows as we make our way down the long Smith School driveway to the large brick pillar gates. Here, we cross a two-lane road to a dark parking lot. In the far back corner, standing out against a copse of trees, is a pink Cadillac. Really pink.

"Are you kidding me?" I ask.

"You have rhinestones on your phone," Izumi points out. That is not the same.

"Used bookstores are a terrible way to make a living," Charlotte says. "Maybe pink was the cheapest color?"

There is no point in explaining that when engaging in clandestine activities, a spy should try to be inconspicuous. Pink is not inconspicuous. But then again, Jennifer is fond of saying, "You get what you get and you don't throw a fit."

This definitely applies to pink Cadillacs.

Chapter 21

DON'T SWEAT THE DETAILS.

THE FIRST THING I REGRET IS the blue sequined dress. For better or worse, we're stuck in our party clothes. Maybe if I wrote down my plans and studied them I'd identify the obvious holes before falling right into them.

The Cadillac, while pink, is also warm and toasty, and we sit quietly three across in the backseat. Bookstore Lady hums along with a country song on the radio. She doesn't ask any questions. Is that because four hundred dollars buys a ride *and* her silence? The dark night races by outside the window.

"So how did you get away from Parker?" I ask to kill time.

"I had to kick him in the shins," Izumi says.

"For real?" Charlotte asks.

"He really likes me," she says. "It's a little intense."

"So you *kicked* him?"

"Well, yeah. I was running out of time. I tried the bathroom excuse, but he followed me, so I had no choice."

"That's the best getaway story ever," Charlotte says with a grin.

Izumi looks at us blankly. "What? What would you have done?"

"Explained nicely that I had to go?" I suggest.

"Told him you were going to be sick and wanted privacy?" Charlotte adds.

Izumi thinks about these. "Nah," she says finally. "Not my style. Once I kicked him, he knew to let me go. And then I stood around waiting for you guys."

"Charlotte was entertaining an audience with the avalanche story," I say.

"Again?" Izumi asks. "Hasn't everyone heard that story a million times already?"

"Not everyone," Charlotte says with a sly smile.

Before we know it, we are pulling into the private jet area at the Hartford airport. Charlotte directs Bookstore Lady to a hangar about a mile from the entrance. It's dark and quiet and no one seems to be around to notice the pink Cadillac creeping down the road. Which is good because between Izumi kicking Parker and the unfortunate color of our getaway car, I'm starting to get nervous. And we haven't even left Connecticut yet. I turn my phone back on and check Monster Mayhem to make sure we are still on track to beat Toby. Unless he develops a way to time-travel, there is no way he arrives before we do.

We climb out of the car at a nondescript airplane hangar. Charlotte thanks Bookstore Lady, and we wave good-bye. The door to the enormous space is open, with dots of light here and there cutting the darkness. A couple of uniformed pilots linger by the stairs leading up to the jet. They are both young men, faces partially obscured by the hats they make pilots wear. And why do they do that? It's not like there's a lot of wind blowing in their faces in the cockpit. And if there is a lot of wind blowing in their faces, that's trouble no hat can fix. But I'm happy they are young and probably don't have kids of their own, otherwise they'd realize this is all sorts of strange.

"Hey, Miss Charlotte," one of them says with a smile as we approach. "Where's Mr. Cavendish?" My heart pounds uncomfortably in my chest. Is this what it feels like when you realize that this time you've maybe gone too far?

"She'd better not tell the avalanche story," Izumi murmurs next to me. I elbow her in the ribs, and she plasters a smile on her face. It's not the avalanche story. It's some nonsense about a charity event that KC *always* brings her to but he's so *busy* and he *really* feels she needs to be there to represent the family and why not bring her friends along because they are all for the cause too? At least it explains our ridiculous outfits.

Without even flinching, the pilots say they're ready for wheels up and usher us onto the plane. It's small but luxurious. I could fall asleep like a cat in a sunbeam. A flight attendant appears.

There's a flight attendant?

"Can I get you ladies anything?" he asks.

Without missing a beat, Charlotte requests Nutella, spoons, and Orangina all around, as if she's done this a million times, which she probably has. The flight attendant disappears behind a curtain, presumably to get us our sugar fix.

We get down to business.

"What do we do when we get there?" asks Izumi.

"And how do we get into the spy college?" throws out Charlotte. "Knock on the door? Ring the bell?"

"How do we find Toby?"

"What if Toby is in the spy college already? How do we stop him? And get him out before anyone finds us?"

"How did you get the plane without anyone knowing, anyway?"

"Easy. I just requested it as KC. He'll never notice."

"Hey, wait a minute," Izumi says. "What if this whole thing is a trap? What if the bad guys are already there waiting?"

"And we're just trying to prevent Toby from chasing after the Skunk Ape, right? We're not there to capture it ourselves?"

"Didn't anyone come up with a plan? Why don't we ever have a plan?"

I hold up my hands. "Okay. Here's the plan. We get to the Blue Diamond Hotel, and we call Veronica."

There is a long, uncomfortable silence while my friends process this information. "Veronica Brooks?" Charlotte asks, indignant. "*The* Veronica Brooks? Are you crazy?"

"She doesn't even like you," Izumi adds.

Thanks for the reminder. "She does like me," I insist. "It's just not the way regular people like other regular people."

"So she doesn't like you," Izumi repeats.

"Be quiet! There's no way we get into the spy college without her."

"But aren't we just going to stop Toby?" Charlotte asks. "Are you *expanding* our mission?" She looks gleeful at this idea, while Izumi frowns.

"Guys, we aren't getting anywhere in figuring out who Micron is, and he's the key in all of this. We need help. And once we tell her Toby's in trouble, I think she will get on board." She always liked Toby better than anyone else.

"And she won't just turn us in?"

Well, this part I'm not so sure about, but I don't want my friends to know, so I nod aggressively. Izumi looks as skeptical as I feel, but there's no other way. I thought about asking Izzie Iceman, but we can't afford her, so that leaves Veronica. We need her. If she won't help us, we're done. Besides, I saved her life once even if she won't admit it. Doesn't she owe me? Somehow I doubt she will find that a compelling reason for breaking every rule in the book and probably some that aren't. But as usual I'm flying by the seat of my pants.

We eat a lot of Nutella and drink a lot of Orangina by the time we touch down at Key West International, a small airport fringed by swaying palm trees. It's ten p.m., but we're on a giant sugar high and wide awake. The pilots seem perfectly happy with Charlotte's standby instructions.

The humid warm air hits us as we exit the plane, and I

take a deep breath. It smells like ocean and hot sand and I immediately want to throw on a swimsuit and crash into the waves. Maybe after we get kicked out of school we can just be beach bums?

We climb into a waiting white stretch limousine, another inconspicuous car, but I know better than to comment. Charlotte is making this happen, and she's making it look easy. Unlike the flight crew, our driver seems a little too concerned that we have no luggage. He keeps murmuring about it as he climbs behind the wheel. It's another detail to add to the pink Cadillac and Parker's bruised shins. It's the kind of detail that will be used against us when those in charge inevitably come looking.

En route, I obsessively check Toby's whereabouts until Charlotte threatens to toss the pink phone out the window. Up until we got on the plane I could see his location clearly. But now the little icon representing his position keeps jumping from place to place, refusing to settle down, like a polarized magnet. There must be interference. At least we know where he's headed.

I slide the phone back under my dress, which is hot and uncomfortable in this climate. I'd give anything for different clothes. Even my horrible Smith School uniform would be an improvement. My feet, swollen from the airplane, no longer even fit in the strappy sandals Charlotte insisted were a "must" with the blue dress, and I kick them off. If at any point we encounter broken glass, I'm in trouble.

It doesn't take long before our limo pulls up in front of the Blue Diamond Hotel. Charlotte shoos the driver away before he can get too curious or uncomfortable about leaving three teenage girls outside a dark hotel in the middle of the night.

There's so much wrong with this situation, it's better if I just don't sweat the details.

Chapter 22

THIS BEACH IS NOT FOR RELAXING.

HUDDLED UNDER A PERFECT swaying palm bulging with coconuts I surely hope don't fall on our heads, we pull up Veronica Brooks, aka Sterling, on the Center's communication network.

"Sterling?" asks Izumi. "Huh?"

"Maybe it's because she never leaves a mess?" I suggest.

"Or she's just supershiny," adds Charlotte.

"I guess we can ask her when we see her," says Izumi. Yes. I'm sure she'll tell us right after she kicks me in the head a few times for having the audacity to show up here. Boy, I really hope she cares about Toby as much as I think she does.

My palms are sweaty as I hit connect. She's going to kill me. I just know it.

Her face appears on the screen. Well, part of her face anyway, but I'd recognize that blue eyeball anywhere. And it's a tired eyeball. One that just got woken up in the middle of the night.

"This better not be you, Hunter," she growls.

"Hi, Veronica," I squeak.

"What do you think you're doing? Where did you get this phone?" She does not sound pleased, and while I knew she wouldn't be, I kind of hoped she just might be anyway.

"I'm totally sorry," I gush. "We'd never have called you if—"

"We?" I can only see her eye, but I'd bet steam is billowing from her ears. I turn the phone slightly so Izumi and Charlotte come into view. "Oh, great. It's the demented Three Musketeers. Where are you? And what do you want?"

"I'm trying to tell you," I say quickly. "We need to talk to you. Toby's in trouble. Real trouble. Big, bad, messy, ugly—"

"Stop it!"

"Sorry. But it's true."

"Where are you guys? My connection is fuzzy."

"On the beach in front of the Blue Diamond," Izumi pipes up. "Where you take all your calls."

I stomp her foot. "Shut. Up."

"You're *here*?" Veronica asks, indignant. "In Florida? Does the headmaster know?"

"Um. No."

"Girls! What's wrong with you? How did you even get here?"

"It's a long story. Pink Cadillac, plane, white limo."

Veronica rolls her one giant eye. "Enough. This just gets worse every time you open your mouth. Don't move. Stay where you are. I'll be there in fifteen minutes. And Abby?"

"Yes?"

"This better be good. This better be the best ever, otherwise you're dead. Got it?"

"Yes, ma'am," I say automatically.

As Veronica disconnects, Charlotte yells out, "See you soon, Sterling!"

I start pacing the small stretch of beach. I haven't seen Veronica since she graduated last year and left for spy college. During our last conversation, I tried to convince her to tell me which girls at Smith were spies. She refused. I think she called me an annoying little brat or something along those lines. However, she smiled when she said it, so my self-esteem remained intact.

But now I'm pushing boundaries. Actually, I've busted

right through all the boundaries. The most humiliating outcome of this misadventure would be for Veronica to immediately turn me over to Jennifer. I might never recover.

A small light appears out on the ocean along with the hum of a boat engine. The boat comes into view, sleek and white, cutting through the night like a shooting star. It pulls alongside a wooden dock that extends out into the water and stops just long enough for a single person to jump off.

Izumi grips my arm. "Tell me again why this is a good idea."

My mouth is dry. I can barely get any air into my lungs. "I don't know," I whisper. "Maybe we should have stayed at Fake Prom?"

"Will you guys relax?" admonishes Charlotte. But even she looks concerned.

Veronica approaches, her long wavy hair billowing theatrically in the breeze, her arms swinging purposefully at her sides. She looks like a shampoo commercial. But the actors in shampoo commercials don't usually look so angry.

We remain huddled on the beach as Veronica jumps off the dock and stalks toward us. We shrink even smaller when she plants herself in front of us, hands on hips.

"*What* are you doing here?" she demands. "And what's with the *dresses*?"

We all start talking at once.

"We were at Fake Prom and stole a plane!" Izumi blurts. "That's why we're dressed weird."

"Toby's in trouble," I babble. "He's hunting a Skunk Ape!"

"We need help, otherwise he's going to end up on trial for treason!" adds Charlotte.

Veronica holds up a hand. "Stop. Quiet. You." She sticks a finger into my chest. "Summarize."

Oh, boy. "Okay. So. Drexel was kidnapped during school meeting by some insane hacker named Micron. Iceman helped us find out his name, but we can't figure out who he is, and the only way to get Drexel back is to play a round of Monster Mayhem 2.0, controlled by Micron, and capture a bunch of, well, you know, *monsters*, except the monsters are all in really crazy places, like behind the *Mona Lisa* and stuff, like Micron is trying to get us busted, and anyway the Skunk Ape is here and Toby is coming to get it and if he's caught breaking into spy college he's going to end up in jail and we're here to save him!"

"Yeah," says Charlotte.

"That's about it," Izumi adds.

There's an uncomfortable silence during which I second-guess my reasons for looping Veronica in. "Is Skunk Ape a code name?" she asks finally.

"No. It's like a smelly bigfoot."

"Not real?"

"Myth."

"So I guess we can be happy about that," she says with a sigh. Suddenly, she squints into the distance. Her hands ball into fists and she lowers her center of gravity.

Something bad is about to happen.

"Get behind me," she whispers. As we start to move, Veronica grabs me by the sequins. "Not you. You're up front with me. Do you remember anything I taught you?" She continues to scan the horizon.

I could lie, but what's the point? She'll find out soon enough. "I kind of remember Crow," I say, referencing a defensive move that involved using my sharp elbow as a beak and pecking my opponent's eyes out.

"You two," she says, not turning.

"Yes?" Izumi and Charlotte say in unison.

"When I say run, you run down the dock, jump in the water, and start swimming away from shore. I don't think they're going to come from that direction. As fast as you can. Got it?"

Swimming? At night? In the ocean? With sharks? I shiver involuntarily. Veronica casts a glance in my direction. "Don't tell me you're afraid of sharks."

"I'm not," I say quickly.

"They're going to come from over there," she says, pointing to a cluster of palm trees.

"The sharks?"

"Abby, you're killing me. No. The opponents."

On cue, the palm trees rustle.

There are three of them, visible only in silhouette. One is tall and thin, one is medium, and one is short and blocky. A matching set. I have nothing with which to defend myself or my friends except for an uncomfortable pair of shoes.

And one very clearly annoyed Veronica.

These guys are toast.

Chapter 23

UNDERESTIMATE VERONICA
AT YOUR OWN PERIL.

VERONICA RELAXES HER SHOULDERS. Her hands dangle loose at her sides. I do the same. It does not make me feel powerful. My heart races. My palms grow slick with sweat.

"Aw, dang," says the short, stocky guy. He wears a Gators cap. "It's a bunch of girls."

"They shouldn't have said that," growls Veronica, under her breath.

"All right, ladies." The tall guy steps into the small pool of light thrown off by a streetlamp. He has a sharp chin and big ears and is spindly like a flamingo. "You're going to have to come with us. Let's go quietly. Don't make a fuss. Get moving."

The medium-size guy, in a downright terrifying Hawaiian shirt, flanks us with Flamingo. Gators comes straight at us. They intend to herd us like cattle.

"Okay," Veronica whispers. "Now. Run!" Izumi and Charlotte take off down the beach toward the long dock.

"Hey!" Flamingo squawks, and charges after them.

"So you want to play *that* way, do ya?" growls Gators. He lunges for Veronica. She steps to the side, and his bulk lands hard in the sand. Hawaiian Shirt grabs my arms from behind. I struggle to break free, but he just holds on tighter. Gators grabs Veronica's ankle and pulls her down. She throws a leg over him and pins him flat, digging into his soft belly with her knee. He thrashes and howls.

"Help your friend!" I yell at Hawaiian Shirt. "She's going to kill him!"

"You think I'm falling for that?" he grunts. "Are you nuts?"

"Don't blame me if Gators ends up dead," I wheeze. This is getting bad. As I struggle, my rhinestone Abby phone slips from my dress. Just as it's about to fall, I grab it. The fancy apps won't help me now. I have to go caveman. As Hawaiian Shirt adjusts his grip, I wiggle my arm free, pivot at the elbow, and smash the phone into his face. It shatters with a sharp *crack*. Hawaiian Shirt's eyes roll back and he slumps into a heap. I just knocked him out! So great! But I ruined my phone. Not so great. It's a bittersweet moment.

"Stop admiring your work," Veronica yells. "Turn around!" When I do, I'm face-to-face with a panting Flamingo. He's wet up to his knees. Before I can react, he grabs me around the neck and squeezes. "You little brats," he hisses. My vision goes instantly wavy. I can just barely make out Veronica, her forearm pressed hard against Gators's throat. Time is important here. Gators needs to pass out ASAP so Veronica can save me or I'm a goner.

Just when I think I'm going down for good, something hits Flamingo hard from behind. He releases me as he flies across the sand.

Izumi!

"That's my best rugby tackle." She grins. Flamingo staggers to his feet, but Charlotte whacks him in the head with a coconut and he collapses a few feet from Hawaiian Shirt. Veronica slowly removes her arm from Gators, and he remains motionless. One. Two. Three. Check.

But this is not a time to celebrate. I can tell from Veronica's face that she's going to critique our performances while it's still fresh, and she will almost certainly find them wanting.

"My reactions were really slow," I say quickly. "And I should never have let Flamingo sneak up on me and—"

Veronica wipes a bead of sweat from her forehead. "You two," she says to my friends, "you were supposed to swim away. Not come back."

They hang their heads. "Sorry," Izumi mutters.

"But," Veronica continues, "it's good you didn't listen to me. You thought for yourselves and did what needed doing. Nice work."

Wait a minute! Veronica has never once told me thinking for myself was an asset. In fact, I'm pretty sure she told me it would get me killed. And she never compliments me. Ever! Instead of relief at being alive, I'm suddenly supremely jealous of Izumi and Charlotte.

"Yeah," I huff. "Thanks." My friends smile like they just won some kind of spy-of-the-year award. Veronica quickly digs through the shorts of three unconscious men and tucks their wallets into the voluminous pockets of her white linen pants. "So who were those guys?"

"No time for that right now," Veronica says, straightening up. "If what you guys tell me about Toby is true, we have no time to lose. Come on!"

As if by magic, the sleek white boat reappears dockside

and we jump on. The captain wears a baseball cap and dark sunglasses even though it's nighttime. This makes me less confident about his piloting ability around all these reefs, but I don't want to be on the beach when our three bad guys wake up either. Veronica shepherds us into seats at the back of the boat, where we gratefully collapse, now on the far side of the earlier adrenaline rush.

"Okay," Veronica says when we are settled. "Tell me everything about Toby and Micron. Don't leave out a single detail. Not one. Got it?"

She sounds so much like Mrs. Smith, I actually experience a small shiver of fear. If Mrs. Smith created protégés exactly like her when she was headmaster, is Jennifer doing the same thing? Will there be mini-Jennifers running around everywhere next year? I shake this bizarre thought from my head and try to concentrate on Veronica's question.

I tell the story from the beginning. Charlotte and Izumi add details as we go. By the time we reach the island, we're mostly done and Veronica is nodding thoughtfully. The island is completely dark. If you didn't know it was here, you'd crash right into it. Where is the spy college? Where are the people? Don't tell me this whole operation is underground like the Catacombs? We're the mole people of clandestine agencies. The boat noses up to a giant concrete structure built into the island, and an enormous slab rises into the night revealing a dark, watery entryway. Mole people. So not kidding.

The boat slips into the opening and the walls grow close. It's a little like Splash Mountain at Disney World, but not in a fun way. Izumi grips my hand, and I loop my arm through Charlotte's.

"It takes some getting used to," Veronica says casually. "I'd hold on for this part."

Suddenly, the boat drops out from under us and we free-fall. Screaming, we cling to one another and wait for gravity to reassert itself. When the boat hits water with a loud slap, my teeth clatter from the vibration.

"Can't you guys just use normal stairs?" I shout, which sets Veronica off on a laughing fit. I look around. The boat floats gently down a tunnel carved out of rock. If there were singing dolls, we could be on the Small World ride. No wonder spy college is so hard to get into. It's just a hopped-up theme park. If I see Cinderella, I'm going to scream.

Finally, we arrive at a watery parking lot full of glossy white boats just like the one we ride in. The captain expertly pulls the boat into a slip (despite the dark sunglasses), and Veronica motions for us to get out.

"It was totally worth this mess just to watch your faces during the drop," she says, snickering.

"I'm glad you're enjoying yourself," I mutter. As for me, I'm tired and hungry, and the wet sequins are making me itch. "Is it possible to get a change of clothes?"

"Soon," says Veronica. "First we have to wake up the director. She's not going to be happy."

We have a unique ability to aggravate people wherever we go, no matter time of day, location, or situation. It's a skill. Not everyone can do this. Following Veronica down a brightly light hallway, I notice rooms off to both sides. Some are signed as training rooms. Others say INSTRUCTION. There's one for interrogation. I hurry past that one. Another hallway to the right has signs for SLEEPING QUARTERS and MESS HALL. Clearly they have the same interior decorator as the Catacombs. The surfaces are sleek and cold as if, in case of a fast getaway, they don't want any shred of evidence to stick. We stop in front of a meeting room.

"I'll leave you guys here and get the director," Veronica says. "This will give me a minute to explain. . . ."

Her voice trails away. Standing at the far end of the hallway are Jennifer and a woman I don't recognize.

And Toby, his head hanging in defeat.

Chapter 24

BUSTED.

SAYING THAT JENNIFER doesn't look happy is an understatement. The unknown woman doesn't look happy either. Izumi and Charlotte jump behind me and hide. This is a good thing to know about them. If we're ever attacked by zombies, my brains will be eaten first.

Veronica is rooted to the ground beside me, her eyes wide. I've never seen her surprised, and it's almost more unnerving than stumbling upon my mother in this hallway. I bet it was the stolen plane that gave us away. So I ask, "What was it?"

"The pink Cadillac," Jennifer says flatly. Of course!

Who gets away in a pink Cadillac? We should have known better, but in our defense, our options were limited. "And the plane. And you don't like sushi. And the vibrating phone tucked into your dress. And that fact that you were at Spring Fling *at all*. Shall I go on?"

"No thank you." Point taken. The stranger lady holds open the door to an empty room. She's average-looking with brown hair to her shoulders and a pencil tucked behind her ear. She holds a small white dog with a big bow in its hair. A gold name tag reads POPPET. The woman strokes the dog absentmindedly with long pointy red fingernails. I find her immediately terrifying. She watches the interaction between Jennifer and me like a hawk.

"It amazes me, Headmaster Hunter," she says, "that you could be so unaware of what is going on in your school. I doubt Headmaster Smith would have been so lax."

They lock eyes. Jennifer looks like her head might explode. "I was well aware of what was going on," she responds.

"Then you certainly have an interesting way of conducting Center business." The woman sniffs. "Unfortunately, I don't have time to hear the details as we have a kidnapping to deal with."

We follow the woman and the poodle to a Catacomb-like

conference room. Everything is stainless steel and white, and a dozen computer monitors cover the far wall. As I shuffle in, I elbow Toby.

"Why did you bolt?" I hiss. "How did you get back here? When did they catch you? Did you really catch a Snallygaster?"

He gives me a noncommittal shrug, refusing to meet my eyes. Suddenly, I'm furious at my friend. We did all this for him, but why did we bother? He doesn't care about us.

"We are so dead," whispers Izumi. And there's that.

"Good evening, students," says the mystery woman, formally. "I'm Director Gladwell. I run the spy college. Headmaster Hunter and I are old friends." She throws an icy smile at Jennifer. Jennifer returns one of equal temperature. Doesn't Jennifer have any actual friends? I worry about her sometimes. These people she hangs out with are not very nice.

"Director," Veronica interjects. "I was on my way to alert you to what's been going on—"

Director Gladwell holds up a hand. "Of course you were, Sterling. Now, girls, tell me everything."

I deliver a version of recent events that I hope is saner than the one I gave Veronica on the beach. But you'd never know it from the look on Director Gladwell's face. When I get to the bit about Micron, Toby's eyes get really big and Gladwell freaks.

"Did you say Micron?"

"Yes."

"The hacker?"

"Yup."

Gladwell glances at Jennifer, who remains stone-faced. "This is a problem. Veronica, bring up the intel on Micron."

Veronica slides behind a keyboard. I feel Jennifer giving me the death stare. I'm so going to get it. My only hope is they need me to save the world or something. Finally, the big screen on the wall fills with news headlines for all the chaos Micron has caused. And Izzie Iceman wasn't lying. He's been busy.

"How do you know the person behind Monster Mayhem 2.0 is Micron?" Director Gladwell demands.

"Iceman told us," Izumi blurts.

Toby wheels around. "Iceman? *The* Iceman? How?"

We glance at one another and smile. Isabel's secret is safe with us.

"That's on a need-to-know basis," I say, "and you don't need to know."

Jennifer rubs her temples. "Iceman? This just keeps getting worse."

But before she can work herself up too much, a sequence of code flashes on one of the giant screens. Toby leaps in the air as if stung by a bee. "Stop! Ronny, go back to that last screen!" Veronica quickly brings up the code. "There! Look!" We all stare blankly at the sequence of letters and numbers. "Don't you see it?"

"Maybe you should explain?" Jennifer suggests.

Toby sighs. What did he do in his short life to be saddled with the likes of us?

"Zachary Hazard," he says quietly.

Jennifer's eyebrows furrow. "And?"

Toby points to a few lines of code. "This stuff," he says. "These sequences. This is what Zachary and I used to mess around with before, when we were trying to . . . hack the Smith network." He looks at his feet. "We were sure there was something suspicious going on at school. Sorry, Headmaster."

"You're forgiven. Go on."

"Anyway, these sequences were kind of our signature." Toby explains how hackers often leave messages or signatures when doing a job because they like the notoriety. "No one really wants to be anonymous," he says. "We, I mean *they*, all want credit, even if it's only from other hackers. Are you sure this code came from Micron?"

Veronica says the intel came with a high degree of confidence, meaning she's pretty sure it's accurate. Director Gladwell looks oddly gleeful. Micron has a name. She pets the Poppet poodle with quick, sharp strokes.

"How wonderful," she says, her eyes bright. "What do we know about this Zachary Hazard?"

"An ex–Smith student," Jennifer says. She doesn't look nearly so happy. "He struggled. His parents, quite well known in Silicon Valley circles, died in a freak ski accident at a resort near Lake Tahoe. Zachary didn't have it easy, but he made poor choices. Ultimately, he was expelled. Toby, do you have anything to add?"

Toby fidgets uncomfortably. "We were friends." He shrugs. "Best friends, I guess. But then he started doing things. Hacking in a way that was more scary than fun. I asked him to stop. I *wanted* him to stop. But he wouldn't. So I told Mrs. Smith."

"And?" Director Gladwell presses. She wants her bad guy to be more fully formed. She does not want him to be a disgruntled kid.

"And he left school and that was it. He never forgave me. We never talked again."

Poor Toby. I want to hug him and tell him Zachary Hazard was not worthy of his friendship, that he has better friends now. No wonder it sometimes feels like he doesn't trust me.

"What happened to him after the expulsion?" asks Gladwell. "Where did he go? What did he do?"

"I didn't know him," Jennifer says. "And I don't know what happened to him. For those details, you'd have to ask Mrs. Smith."

Director Gladwell rolls her eyes and squeezes Poppet. Poppet grunts. "Fabulous. You and Lola in the same week. I'm obviously being punished for something I did in a past life."

For the first time in a while, Jennifer smiles.

Chapter 25

AND FINALLY, A MISSION!

I WANT OUT OF THIS DRESS. I want to go to sleep. I want a cheeseburger. But mostly I want to know what's going on. Jennifer and Director Gladwell are out in the hallway having a heated discussion. It's been going on for at least ten minutes. We sit in the conference room with Veronica, who quietly simmers, and Toby, who's as bedraggled as a wet dog.

"I can't believe you hitchhiked down here," I tell him. "That's dangerous."

"I can't believe you broke into my room and stole the Abby phone! It wasn't ready."

"I had no choice," I sniff. I decide to save the bit about

smashing the phone against some guy's head until later.

"And you stole a plane," Toby adds.

"It was way easy," Charlotte throws out.

"Why did you ditch us at the *Mona Lisa*?" asks Izumi.

"Can you guys just leave me alone?"

"No," I say.

"Who's Iceman?" he shoots back.

"We're never telling," Izumi says. Izzie would surely have us killed if we did.

"Fine," Toby says. "I needed a distraction to get the Quinotaur in the *Mona Lisa* room, so I fried the security camera and I pulled the fire alarm."

"You. Did. Not," says Charlotte.

"Yeah."

"I'm a little dazzled," Izumi says, and Toby grins.

"It was pretty good."

No, it wasn't. He didn't tell us any of it. He went all freelance and rogue and just left us standing around wondering if he was dead or alive. Toby stops smiling.

"Sorry, Abby," he mutters. "I was going to tell you guys, but I thought it was better if I went it alone. I just mess things up when it comes to friends."

"We're not Zachary Hazard," I say sharply.

His face falls. "No," he says. "You're not."

And I feel bad. Toby doesn't have the greatest luck when it comes to friends. But we're *different*. "We're in this together. Trust us. Please."

"Yeah," adds Charlotte. "Zachary's a bad dude. We're not."

"Dudes *or* bad," Izumi clarifies.

"You guys are killing me," Veronica says, rolling her eyes.

And Toby laughs, a real belly laugh that seems to rise from the soles of his feet. It's infectious, and soon we are laughing with him, even Veronica. Maybe it's the exhaustion. Or maybe it's stress. Or maybe it's just relief that we are all back on the same page.

Not that it's a nice page. The idea of revenge makes sense. Zachary is putting Toby in situations where a monster capture almost requires a miracle while his father's life hangs in the balance. He is torturing Toby for his own amusement, like a cat playing with a wounded, blind mouse. And somehow that's scarier than the usual bad-guy motives of total world domination.

Jennifer and Director Gladwell burst into the room, and we abruptly stop laughing. Director Gladwell is red in the face, and Jennifer scowls. Even the poodle seems alarmed. Veronica pops to her feet at attention, but the director barely glances at her. She's too busy glaring at Jennifer.

"We find ourselves in an uncomfortable situation," Jennifer says tightly. *Tell me about it. This dress is killing me.* Izumi squeezes my hand so hard I yelp. "You four have broken every rule. You've been incredibly, stupidly casual with your own lives. You've betrayed every possible trust and confidence. I'm so angry I want to scream. And I *never* scream. But . . ." Will we be saved by the "but"? Is it even possible given our trespasses? The room goes deathly quiet. I hold my breath. "It seems in light of current circumstances, we *need* your expertise. No one in the Center's organization knows Monster Mayhem like you do."

Oh, I love being needed! Izumi releases my hand. Our execution has been stayed, at least temporarily. I'm sure the hammer will come down later, but for now we're necessary. Important. Crucial. Required. I squirm in my seat.

"We have two goals. Capture Micron, aka Zachary Hazard, and get Drexel Caine home safely. Our advantage is that Zachary doesn't know that we are onto him. Nothing in the intelligence indicates otherwise."

"The element of surprise," Director Gladwell adds. "And we will use this to our advantage. Toby, you will continue to play the game exactly as you have been. Eventually, this will lead us to Zachary Hazard. Girls, you are his backup. His support team. You help him play the game. Got it?

Hazard cannot know that anything has changed."

We're going undercover as ourselves, as a team? How cool. "Does this mean we're officially part of the Center?" I ask.

"Don't push it, missy," Jennifer growls. And somehow I just know this plan is not her idea.

"Okay. Okay," I say. "I'm good. No problem."

"We'll have a proper debriefing tomorrow at oh six hundred hours—" Director Gladwell says.

"Maxine," Jennifer interrupts. "These kids are thirteen. Can you just use the regular clock?"

Maxine, who I guess is the same person as Director Gladwell, shoots Jennifer a deadly look. "Six o'clock in the morning," she says curtly. "That will give everyone a few hours of sleep. Don't be late. I can't abide late."

"Ma'am?" pipes up Veronica from the back of the room. "What are my orders?"

"Oh, you're in this, Sterling," Gladwell says. "You're deep in this. Be here at six, ready to roll. You'll be point on this mission."

We have a mission! A real live actual mission! The scary director just said so. I know if I jump for joy, Jennifer will clobber me, so I try to keep my excitement under wraps, but there's a real possibility I might explode. Veronica doesn't look as happy as I am. "But, ma'am," she says. "I was leading the effort on the Bulgarian . . ."

Director Gladwell cuts her off with a glance. "Not anymore," she says. "Now you're up to your elbows in *children*." She gathers up her poodle, pausing in front of us. "And by the time this is over, you will reveal Iceman's identity."

"Death first," Charlotte responds, a little too casually for my taste. Gladwell glares at her. Jennifer steps between us.

"Remember that time I shot you?" Jennifer asks Gladwell.

Gladwell's eyes narrow. "You should have been removed from duty."

"I *should* have aimed better."

Chapter 26

WAITING FOR A MESSAGE.
AND WAITING. AND WAITING.

VERONICA LEADS THE four of us to our quarters. Along the way, she mutters. "I should know that if it involves Abby Hunter it's trouble. Why did I answer that call? Now Bulgaria, the mission that was going to get me *noticed*, is gone. Just like that, poof, I'm back to babysitting. This is a nightmare. A nightmare that won't end. Yup, I'm stuck in a recurring nightmare with a bunch of junior high kids. I could cry. Seriously."

I catch up to her. "I'm really sorry," I say. "I didn't mean for this to happen."

Veronica wheels around on me, eyes blazing. "You never mean for *anything* to happen."

I slide back to my trailing friends. "She's totally angry," I whisper.

"And you're surprised?" asks Charlotte.

"Not really," I say.

Our quarters are four bedrooms surrounding a common area that looks like an uncomfortable living room. Veronica does not even come all the way in.

"Six o'clock," she says. "Don't be late."

We're alone for the first time since the beach. There's no one obvious watching. We stare at one another.

"We have a mission!" I shriek.

"I can't believe it!"

"This is *insane!*"

"Do you think we'll get kicked out of school *after* the mission is over?" Izumi asks.

"They seem pretty excited to have a line on Micron," I say. "We might get away with it. I mean, I'm sure we'll be scrubbing pots or sorting uniforms or something, but we won't be expelled. At least not for this."

Toby doesn't seem to share our excitement. "I can't believe Zachary hates me this much," he says quietly. "I was trying to help him, trying to stop him before he went too far."

I sit down next to him. "It's not you," I say. "You did

everything right. It's him. And we're going to help the Center make sure he can't do this, or any of his other crazy stuff, again. We're on a mission."

"We're on a mission!" Charlotte yells.

And this time, Toby smiles. "Hey, you guys need to calm down. And what's with the dresses?"

"Fake Prom," I remind him.

"Oh wow, I totally forgot."

"It was awful."

"It wasn't *that* bad," Izumi says with a shrug.

"We should go to bed," I say. Who knows what sort of madness Maxine will have cooked up for us by morning?

Before we split into different rooms, Toby says, "Thanks, you guys, for being part of my team." He closes his door before we can tell him we're glad he's on our team too. We all have different strengths, and that's what makes us good together. Sometimes the trouble is recognizing that.

I'm asleep before my head hits the scratchy white pillow.

The morning comes as a shock, but not because we got no sleep and are in an underground bunker. We're Center agents! I leap out of bed and put on a pair of neatly folded cargo pants and a clean sweatshirt that were already in the room. There is nothing exciting about the clothes, but my other option is the blue sequined dress lying in a sad heap in the corner. Last night seems so long ago. I wander out into the common area to find Toby hunched over a laptop, holding a steaming mug of coffee.

"No one cares if you drink coffee here," he says without looking at me.

I flop down next to him. On his screen is a larger version of the Monster Mayhem 2.0. He stares at it intently.

"What are you doing?" I ask after a minute.

"Waiting."

"For what?"

He looks at me like I'm a complete idiot. "The next *message*. I caught the Skunk Ape. What's next?"

"Oh, right," I say. "Of course. Won't Zachary know you're hanging out here?"

Toby shakes his head. "They scramble all the signals here. On the outside, it probably looks like I'm in Miami. This place is top-notch." That explains why I couldn't pinpoint him before.

"It they're so good at stuff, why can't they just locate Zachary and go and get him?"

Toby gives me another *my friend is a dope* look. "Because Zachary is not *in* the game. Only I am. We can't even tell what country he's in because he's covered all his tracks."

Well, good for Zachary. Toby slurps down some coffee. "You're not ever going to tell me who Iceman is, are you?"

"No," I say. He sighs. I sit beside my friend, in silence, staring at the screen until that gets really boring, and then I go and wake up the girls, who are not excited to see me.

Veronica isn't excited to see me either. She leads us to another conference room, and this one has a decent spread of bagels and cream cheese on the table. But my mouth is kind of dry and the bagel gets stuck.

Maxine Gladwell yawns and tries to hide it with her hand. Jennifer's shoulders sag. Even Poppet the poodle has bags under his eyes. Director Gladwell asks us to sit down. The lights dim, and a big photograph of Bad Beret fills the screen.

"Wait a minute," I yelp. "I've seen him before! He was stalking Toby! *Bad Beret* is Zachary Hazard?" Unfortunately, I'm forced to tell the story of how I followed Zachary in the Paris hotel.

Jennifer rolls her eyes. "Of course you followed him," she mutters.

"He wasn't happy," I point out.

"No," Jennifer says. "Happy, well-adjusted people don't usually go around perpetrating kidnappings."

"Can we continue?" asks Director Gladwell, miffed. "Our analysts believe that Drexel Caine's kidnapping and Hazard's game of revenge are part of a larger plot. What that plot is, we can't be sure. We'll keep sifting through the data. For now, what we're going to do is simple. We wait for the next message, and we follow Zachary's instructions to the letter. You four are now officially on loan from Smith. Agent Sterling will be your minder." Real spies have handlers. We have a minder. Definitely not as cool. "Remember Toby is meant to be acting alone. Zachary will believe that he brought in his friends. That's plausible. But he must not find out about the Center's involvement. Veronica will be your *only* point of contact. You are not to reach out to the Center in any other way. If you do, the whole mission could fail. But rest assured, while you may not see us, we are there."

Where have I heard that before? Forgive me if this does not give me confidence. I exchange a look with Izumi and Charlotte. They agree. "So now what?" I ask.

"Now we wait for the next message," says Director Gladwell. I was afraid of that. I hate waiting. "But we should take advantage of the time and get some things squared away. Veronica, take them to Angus so he can get them outfitted. And then maybe a few rounds in the training room?"

Training room? Oh please, not that. Anything but that! As Veronica herds the four of us out of the conference room, Jennifer grabs me.

"Abby will join you in a minute," she says, pulling me down the hallway to an empty room. She shuts the door quietly, and for the first time since this began, I'm truly afraid. The punishments Jennifer has at her disposal are limitless.

"You're in big trouble," she says immediately.

"I know. I'm sorry."

"Well, lucky for you, punishment will have to wait, because we have bigger fish to fry. I'm going back to Smith, but Director Gladwell is close to the best. She'll make sure things go according to plan."

"I thought you didn't like her."

"Oh, she's a pain in the neck, but that doesn't mean she's bad at her job. It's hard work, what she does. I wouldn't want to do it. I don't even want to be headmaster of Smith." She sighs before realizing we're no longer talking about me. "Anyway, that's not a conversation for right now. Right now you need to be good. *Listen.* No going off plan. Do you understand how important this is?"

Yes. It's about saving the world.

Chapter 27

WATER BOTTLES AND EXPLODING CHAPSTICKS.

AFTER MY MOTHER GIVES me a slightly too long hug and reminds me five more times to listen to my instructions and not go rogue, I scurry to catch up with my friends. Along the way, I peek in different doors and windows. In one room, I see a dozen students doing martial arts training. In another, they practice Mandarin. In yet another, they appear to be defusing a fake bomb, a giant countdown clock in the middle of the wide table, challenging them to go faster.

After getting horribly lost, I beg directions from a terrifyingly buff spy in training who says Angus is on sublevel A, in the "bunker." But this whole place is a bunker! I may never be heard from again.

Finally, I stumble through a set of swinging doors into a long concrete box that definitely could be a bunker. Along each wall are floor-to-ceiling metal shelves stacked with plastic bins and cardboard boxes. They overflow with cables and wires and look a lot like angry octopuses. The space is narrow but endless, an entire sea of tentacled creatures. My footsteps echo on the cold, gray floor, but otherwise it's silent. Where is everyone?

Suddenly, I hear Toby scream, "That is so cool!" and I follow his voice to a small space between the shelving. Clustered around a worktable littered with electronic debris, under bright lights, are my friends and a man who must be Angus.

I was not expecting Angus. I'm not sure anyone could ever expect Angus. If the ceilings in here are about ten feet high, Angus must be seven feet tall, even with the old-guy stoop. He has wild white hair, possibly styled by sticking his head out the window while he drove to work. His eyebrows are woolly caterpillars creeping slowly toward each other with plans to meet in the middle. Big blotches of neon orange and yellow stain his lab coat, the breast pocket of which is so full of pencils, the seams strain. In short, Angus looks like a madman.

But my friends find him so captivating that they don't even notice when I arrive. "Oh hi, Abby," Charlotte finally says. "This is Angus, and he is *way* cool."

"Ah, the legendary Abigail Hunter." Angus extends a hand. I can see a spiderweb of blue veins under his skin. "Oh, wait a minute. It's your mother that's a legend. Never mind. Welcome to the lab anyway." Jeez, what a start.

"I could just stay here forever," Izumi says, gazing at the pile of junk on the table.

"Me too," says Toby wistfully.

"What's all this stuff?" I ask. There are ordinary items, things I might carry around in my backpack: a ChapStick, a collapsible water bottle, a pair of sunglasses, a nail file, nail polish, a fancy pen, an ordinary pencil, a roll of Life Savers, a silver bookmark, and some other things.

"Magic," sighs Charlotte.

"Yeah," Toby agrees.

"We're happy to have you join us, Abby," Angus says. "Even if you're not Jennifer."

Here's the thing about having a famous mother. It's mostly just annoying. I have yet to find an upside. "Glad I found you," I say flatly. Angus guffaws loudly, snorts a few times, and slaps his thigh. I have no idea what's so funny.

"Check this out," Izumi says. She picks up the ordinary pencil and jabs me hard with the eraser end. A bolt of electricity shocks my shoulder, and I go flying backward into the shelves.

"Ouch!"

Izumi giggles. "And that was set to low. Boy, it must stink to get hit with it on high."

"It can be rather uncomfortable," says Angus. "And remember it doesn't work without the pressure. It must make contact with the intended victim. And keep it out of water." He closes his eyes and shudders. "That can be . . . messy."

I get back on my feet and rub the instant bruise left behind. "Thanks," I grumble.

"How about this?" Charlotte aims a shiny black pen at the wall and out shoots a dark blue liquid. It fizzles and spits when it hits the concrete and quickly begins to eat it away. A shocking pencil and an acid-filled pen.

I learn the ChapStick explodes, the sunglasses are night-vision goggles, the nail polish is a super adhesive, the nail file kit is for lock picking, the Life Savers destroy gas tanks and incapacitate cars, the silver bookmark is a communication disruptor, and the water bottle is just that, a water bottle. Apparently, even spies need to hydrate.

"Now that I have you all here," Angus says, "let's get the standard-issue stuff out of the way. For this mission, I'm told you will be wearing street clothes, so the technical uniforms are not necessary."

"What are they?" Toby asks.

"Oh, you know, clothing that helps you blend in, be invisible. Some of the outfits have built in survival mechanisms, floatation, fireproofing, that sort of thing. And we're working on garments that communicate with you about your own body and directly with the Center as well. I'm particularly excited about those suits."

"Isn't your brain supposed to be in charge of communicating with your body?" I ask.

This makes Angus laugh again. "Oh, you're a silly one," he says, patting me on the head. "What I mean is your suit can tell you the extent of a sustained injury. As in, are you able to go on and complete the mission or are you better off just surrendering to the bad guy and getting it over with?" He grins maniacally, pulling a few multicolored backpacks off the shelves. Izumi gets camouflage. Toby gets a preppy-looking navy one. Charlotte's is a hip orange. And mine is pink. Really? My friends snicker.

"How did you know that's her favorite color?" Toby laughs.

"I have a knack," Angus says, waggling his woolly eyebrows. "Now, each backpack comes equipped with all this gear. But I've been working on something new." He pulls out four half-size Pringles containers. Snacks?

"The Cement Shoes A402!" Toby exclaims. "I tried to make one in my dorm room. It was a disaster."

"You need to calibrate it just right," Angus instructs. "It's persnickety."

"Excuse me," I interrupt. "Does that mean there are no chips in the can?"

"Toby, why don't you demonstrate? Remember, you have to remove the plastic lid and toggle the switch to arm it."

In one swift motion, leaving me no time to run, Toby launches the Pringles container at my feet. It bounces off my shoes, and suddenly I can't move, my feet encased up to midcalf in a fast-hardening gray substance that does look a lot like cement. I immediately fall over backward. Numbness creeps up my legs. But panicking is more embarrassing than being laid low by a can of Pringles.

"I did not give you permission to experiment on me!" I howl. The numbness spreads. Angus regards me casually.

"I added a substance that temporarily paralyzes your prey," he says. "It's nothing permanent, so no need to be alarmed."

Great. No big deal. I'm just wearing cement shoes and I'm paralyzed. Toby grins. "Awesome idea."

"That is so excellent!" Izumi jumps up and down. I've never seen her this excited, aside from when Parker asked her to Fake Prom.

Charlotte approaches and pokes curiously at the cement shoes, which grow harder by the second. I can no longer feel my arms. "How long does it last?" she asks.

"Forever," Angus says with a shrug.

What? I'd cry, but I can't feel my face. "Of course, I have the release formula. Hold on a minute." He pats the pockets of his white jacket like an absentminded professor. "Oh, here it is!" He pulls out a little glass vial. "Now we just sprinkle it here and there and it sets off a chemical reaction. . . ."

Suddenly, I'm steaming and fizzing like the Wicked Witch of the West. I close my eyes and prepare to scream, but the shoes simply melt away. I wiggle my fingers and toes. Everything is back to normal except for my pride. I point a finger at Toby. "Do *not* do that again."

"Focus, friends," Angus chides. "We have much to

cover." He pulls several slim pieces of plastic, about the size and width of a credit card, from one of his many pockets. "Now, this is a very old-school tracker and one of my favorites. It's gotten many an agent out of a tight spot in the past. These days I worry that you young people want slick at the expense of practical. If it doesn't beep or buzz or hum, you aren't interested. But keep in mind that sometimes simple is best." From another pocket, he pulls a bunch of rubber bracelets in iridescent colors that change as the bracelet catches the light. Charlotte grabs one and immediately uses it to create a messy ponytail on the top of her head.

"Perfect," she says.

"Go get lost," instructs Angus.

"Pardon me?"

"Go hide. You're helping me demonstrate."

"Oh! I get it. Okay." She takes off down the aisle between the shelving until we can no longer see her in the shadows.

"Now," says Angus, "the chip that talks to the tracker is in the bracelet." He presses his thumb to a space on the card that glows green beneath his touch. "Give it a minute and it will return exact coordinates of the person wearing the bracelet."

Within seconds, a series of green numbers move across

the surface of the card. Toby practically drools. "Radio waves?" he asks timidly.

"Something like that," Angus says with a wink. "It doesn't rely on cell networks or Wi-Fi. It needs infrequent charging. Brilliant, if I do say so myself, and I invented it! Then you just ask it to translate the coordinates to an address and you can pinpoint your person. Keep those bracelets on. You never know when one of you will need finding."

"This is great and all," I say. "But what about phones?"

"Phones are dangerous," Angus says grimly. "They are porous and hackable and unreliable, and you become dependent and stupid. You stop looking around and only look down. And then you get yourself killed."

Toby looks positively mortified that his new hero could say such a thing.

"So that's a no?" Charlotte asks for clarification.

"The only phone on this mission will be Toby's, as it is necessary for playing the game." Case closed. We will go forth phoneless. This is hard to take. There's a lot of exaggerated sighing.

When Angus is finally satisfied that we're not going to accidentally blow each other up or cement shoe ourselves or electrocute the innocent, we head to his office so he can sign all the equipment out to us.

Behind Angus's large, messy desk is a sturdy glass case in which is mounted a shiny silver disc about the size of an ashtray. A light illuminates a series of symbols and lines carved on its surface. It's oddly beautiful.

"The cipher," Angus says. "My prized possession."

"Cipher?" asks Charlotte.

"A cipher is a disguised way of writing," he answers. "A code, if you will. This one is from the early 1400s. It belonged to a duke in what is now northern Italy." He pulls it out gently and holds it for us to see. "These symbols correspond to letters so you can translate messages. But you need the cipher on both ends, to write and read." He gazes at us. "Humanity has been spying since the beginning of time. I wonder what it would be like if we didn't have to."

Chapter 28

A HOBGOBLIN IN LONDON.

THE REST OF THE DAY we sit around and stare at Toby's phone. We mentally urge it to deliver a message so we can get on to the fun part. Veronica tells us we're idiots for thinking there is a fun part.

"This is not about fun," she says. "This is about saving the world." I wish people would stop saying that. Every time they do, I feel a little sick.

We play a few rounds of Uno and one long game of Monopoly, where no one wins and Charlotte steals from the bank. Every fifteen minutes or so, someone pops a head in and asks for an update. We have nothing to report except that Charlotte cheats at Monopoly. They don't seem to care about that.

We eat lunch in the cafeteria with all the other spy college students. We don't so much as warrant a glance. Veronica refuses to sit with us. She says babysitting duty did not specifically include meals. Besides, she can see us perfectly from her table of friends twenty feet away. Toby's phone occupies the center of the table like a centerpiece and in between bites we wonder aloud how long we're going to be stuck here doing nothing.

"It could be worse," Izumi says. "We could be in class right now."

We agree that's true. Maybe sitting here staring at the phone isn't so bad. But really, it is that bad. *Nothing* is happening.

Finally, at four fifteen, when we are about to lose our collective minds . . . *PING*. We leap up from the common area chairs and simultaneously lunge for the phone. Toby gets it first, and we swarm him.

"Is it him?"

"What does it say?"

"Do we get out of here now?"

"Hurry up and read it!"

"Can you guys give me some space, please?" Toby asks, turning his back on us, which is a little bit annoying because even though it's his phone, it's *our* mission. "So I guess we're going to . . . London?"

That's it. We tackle him and snatch the phone. A map of London fills the Monster Mayhem screen. *Go with great haste—there's no time to waste!* Because we've been sitting here for a day, Toby's health is low. We're going to have to pit-stop to bag a Cyclops or a Chimera or something before we go off to London hunting Hobgoblins. We probably should have eaten a better lunch.

Veronica bursts into the room. "You got it?" Toby nods, his eyes blazing. Veronica studies the screen. Her eyebrows furrow. "London. Okay. Director Gladwell is waiting for us. Come on."

En route, we explain about having to catch a monster to keep our health up. Veronica does not like this at all. She says there must be something wrong with us if we think this game is fun. But I'm not sure Veronica would know fun if it kicked her in the shins.

Director Gladwell's office doesn't have any windows either. I'm reconsidering if spy college will be a good fit for me. I like daylight. The director sits behind an enormous desk, stroking Poppet the poodle and smiling in a way that makes me squirm. "The plane is making preparations," she says. "We should have you there in no time to begin your mission."

"What exactly *is* our mission?" I ask. "The details and stuff?"

"I was getting to that. Why not practice a little patience? You *do* remind me of your mother."

And that is not a good thing, I'm guessing.

"Your mission is to follow Zachary's instructions and give him no cause for suspicion. We will handle everything else. You are under no circumstances to deviate from these instructions. We follow the rules around here. Is that understood?"

"Perfectly, ma'am," Veronica says in a loud, clear voice. The rest of us mumble our agreement.

"Sterling, you're in charge on the ground and . . ."

Charlotte's hand shoots up, earning a withering glare from the director. "Yes?"

"Do we get code names?" asks Charlotte. "Everyone has them. I thought I might be Diamond or Titanium. What do you think?"

"I *think* you should be quiet and listen." Poppet gives us a smug little look as the director adjusts the dog's pink sweater. "Now, Sterling."

"Yes, ma'am?"

"The normal communication protocols apply. I understand you view this mission as babysitting, but it's far beyond that. We need you to be precise."

"Yes, ma'am. Absolutely. You can count on me."

"I *know* that," Gladwell says, annoyed. "Just don't screw up." Veronica maintains a perfectly neutral expression. If she's bothered by Gladwell's words, she doesn't show it. I'm not sure I'll ever be that good. "Sterling will also be in charge of Toby's phone."

"What?" This is the first thing Toby has said since entering the director's chambers. Turns out he's awake after all.

"It's our only means of communicating with Zachary, and I'm not leaving it in the hands of a kid. If there's one thing kids can be counted on for, it's to mess things up. Honestly, I don't know how Mrs. Smith did it for so long. It's no wonder she snapped. Sterling gets the phone. End of discussion."

Veronica gives Toby a sympathetic look as he begrudgingly hands over the phone. "I'll take good care of it," she whispers. Toby nods but casts his eyes to the floor. His very tenuous link to his dad has just been broken. Anxiety and frustration rise off him in waves. Director Gladwell doesn't notice. "Muster on the airstrip in thirty minutes," she says. "Don't be late. Don't forget anything." With that, she shoos us out of her office like the little brats she obviously thinks we are.

"She's not very nice," Izumi whispers the minute we hit the hallway. "We should call Jennifer and complain."

Veronica sighs, but possibly for the first time the exasperation is not directed at me. "That won't help. The best we can do is follow her instructions." And with a wink, she hands Toby back his phone.

A big grin spreads across Toby's face. "Sure," he says. "We'll follow the instructions *exactly*."

"Wait," says Charlotte. "So are we now cool with breaking the rules?"

"No," Izumi and I say together.

"Okay, okay, calm down. I had to check."

"Listen, my sweet and innocent friends," Veronica says with some menace. "This is not a joke. In my opinion, Toby is the best one to have the phone and communicate with Zachary. It's what Zachary is expecting, and part of what we're meant to do is keep him believing that no one's the wiser. I'm just doing my job."

And that is the end of that. We follow Veronica back to our quarters, collect our multicolored backpacks, and hurry up to "muster" before we get in trouble for being late.

Chapter 29

MY JET LAG HAS JET LAG.

I CAN'T BELIEVE we've crossed the Atlantic Ocean for the second time in two weeks. Even Charlotte is puffy after this flight. We yawn and stagger after Veronica, who strides toward the terminal exit with a ridiculous amount of energy. How does she do that?

Outside it's gray and a light rain falls. A black sedan with tinted windows pulls immediately to the curb, and Veronica indicates we should get in. We cram in the backseat while she takes the front.

The driver greets her like an old friend, and there's some laughing about her babysitting job. Word sure travels fast. After a while, we cruise slowly down a cobblestone alley before stopping in front of a small brick building. The blinds are drawn tight across the dark upstairs windows. The place looks cold and unwelcoming, and this applies to the inside as well.

"Stark," says Izumi, glancing around the first level of the house.

"Empty," adds Charlotte.

Both are true. There's a rickety table with four chairs and not much else.

"What is this place?" I ask.

"Safe house," Veronica says. "They all look like this."

"Why does being safe have to be uncomfortable?" Charlotte asks. Before Veronica can answer, a loud pounding at the front door interrupts us.

"Our host," says Veronica wryly.

We keep adding people to this party. Soon we're going to be identifiable from the moon. After an exchange of secret code words that I can't decipher (cow? Apple blossoms in May?), in walks a tall lanky woman around Veronica's age, with a cascade of shiny black hair tumbling down her back. She wears reflective aviator sunglasses even though it's raining and a plaid Burberry trench coat cinched tightly at the waist.

Toby falls madly in love. I watch it happen. For some

reason, it bothers me. So what if this stranger is beautiful? Can she stop bad guys?

"Welcome to Bloomsbury," the beautiful stranger says with a crisp accent. Toby swoons. Seriously. How can he be thinking about girls when his father is in grave danger? I give him a nudge and furrowed eyebrows. He ignores me. "This is a lovely neighborhood with many cultural sites and beautiful gardens. We're glad to host our American friends. I'm to offer any logistical support you might require. Oh, and I'm Xena."

Of course you are.

"Thank you, Xena," Veronica says. "Our mission is fairly straightforward, as you know, but we always appreciate support."

It's like they're reading from a script. It's weird. Charlotte raises a hand. "Um, excuse me, Xena?"

Xena finally removes her sunglasses. Her dark eyes settle on Charlotte. "Yes?"

"*Where* did you get your coat? I love it. It's amazing." Apparently, Charlotte's in love too. Fabulous. Without answering, Xena turns a withering glare on Veronica, who blushes beet red.

"They're new, unseasoned," Veronica explains quickly, "but necessary to the success of this mission. As you know,

Micron is not your everyday threat. We need to make allowances for breaches in protocol such as this."

Since when was paying someone a compliment a breach in protocol? No one mentioned any protocol to us. Maybe if they did we wouldn't breach it. This encounter is giving me a bad taste in my mouth. If we're expected to be unseasoned, protocol-breaching brats, well, let's do it.

"I'm hungry," I whine. "And thirsty. And tired. And I'm getting a little bored."

Xena looks like I just sucker punched her. Veronica looks like she might sucker punch me. Charlotte giggles. Izumi does too. Toby gazes upon Xena like she's Aphrodite come to life.

"You certainly have your work cut out for you," Xena says with disgust. "The kitchen is stocked. Our apologies about the level of cleanliness. We did not receive much notice before your arrival. Please do let me know if I can be of further service. Sterling, you know how to reach me."

"Yes," says Veronica, escorting Xena to the door. "Thank you. We will."

With Xena gone, Veronica finally exhales. "Thanks, guys," she says. "You were really terrific." Somehow I don't think she means it.

"Is everyone in the spy community grouchy?" asks Izumi.

"Yes," hisses Veronica. "Mean and grouchy. It's the way things are. Grab something to eat, and then I'm putting you through your paces. Let's do a little training and see how grouchy and mean you are when we're done. " With that, she grabs her bag and stomps up the narrow stairs.

"What does she mean by 'paces'?" Izumi whispers.

"It means she's going to beat us up," I say.

"It's training," Toby says, finally breaking out of his trance.

"'Training' is just a nice way of saying she's going to beat us up," I say. "Trust me. I know what I'm talking about. We'd better find some chocolate to fortify ourselves."

Thirty minutes later, as instructed, we sit in a large upstairs room with a glossy wooden floor and mirrored walls. It does not resemble the rest of this austere house at all. But it does remind me of the room where I first experienced Veronica's "training."

I advise my friends not to complain. "Complaining just makes it worse," I explain. "And watch out for her right foot. It's vicious. If that foot makes contact with your body, you are going to wish you were back in Mr. Chin's Chinese History 2 class."

"No way," says Charlotte.

"So, any actual advice?" Izumi asks.

Run? Hide? Beg for mercy? Request asylum here in the United Kingdom?

"Sometimes if I concentrate really hard on something else," I say, "like a good book or—"

"Or that awesome coat," Charlotte interrupts.

"Or Xena," Toby adds.

"Parker," throws in Izumi.

"Sure," I say. "Whatever is distracting. It helps get you centered and you defend yourself and fight better. At least it works that way for me."

"Did you say 'fight'?" Izumi asks, her dark eyes glittering.

"Um, yes?"

"Cool."

"No," I say, shaking my head. "It's not cool. It's awful, and you don't want to be in a situation where you have to do it, because that's scary."

"But I kind of do," Izumi counters.

"I don't," Charlotte says.

"Me either," says Toby. "I'm way better fighting from behind a keyboard."

I think about the fight I had in the snow last year with a cute boy who actually turned out to be bad. I used what Veronica taught me. There was a purpose to the harsh training she put me through. Sure, I can warn my friends, but until they experience it themselves, it won't have any meaning.

Veronica enters the room. She's back in the flowing white linen pants and a dark T-shirt. Her blond hair is piled up in a messy bun on top of her head. Her eyes are steely. Toby swallows a few times. I get it. My mouth is dry too.

"I never have much time with you, do I?" she muses, looking at me. "There's always a crisis and there you are. If we weren't on the same side, you'd have all the makings of a perfect nemesis." I'll admit that kind of hurts my feelings. I brace myself for what comes next. "Okay, you innocent youngsters, remember this is about self-defense, not aggression. Try and keep up."

With that, she shoots her foot out, positioning her heel behind mine and pulls, and I'm down on the hardwood floor staring up at the ceiling.

"That's called the Heel Sweep," she says. "It's good for tight spaces." I wish that gave me comfort. I leap to my feet, my stance low and my hands up, ready to defend the barrage of blows I know are incoming. Veronica's fists fly. She strikes my palms, lands a few jabs to my upper arms and the soft part of my stomach. She reels off a round-house kick that throws me off balance, and I stumble. The sole of her foot comes down hard on my back and flattens me like a pancake. And for a minute there, I thought I was doing pretty well.

I roll out from under her and hop back up. Sweat runs down my back. Veronica isn't even breathing that hard. Eyeballing me with a sly grin, she slides along the slick floor and scissors my legs with hers. I go over again, this time landing hard on my knees. I bite my tongue to keep from yelping. No reason to antagonize her.

"Get up," she commands. I struggle back to my feet. My heart pounds with the exertion. Toby stands with his back pressed to the wall, mouth hanging open. Charlotte studies her cuticles. Only Izumi watches intently.

The next five minutes are a series of blows, 50 percent of which I block, 50 percent of which land perfectly on my now-battered body. We are about to embark on a world-saving mission, and I really just don't see how this is helping. Honestly, I think Veronica is doing this purely for her own amusement. I am not enjoying myself. Maybe this whole spy thing isn't for me after all. I might end up being good at it, but is that the same as *liking* it? Not really. In truth, Izumi was right about the grouchiness. No one seems overjoyed about being a spy. They are either annoyed or suspicious or both. Where's the fun in that? If there is any, I'm not seeing it.

"Go Abby!" I hear from the side of the room. Izumi claps her hands. I look down. I have Veronica pinned under my foot. I have no idea how this happened. I immediately drop to my knees beside her.

"Are you okay?" I whisper, touching her gently on the shoulder. "I didn't mean to . . . I mean, I don't know what happened. . . . I was just thinking about how being a spy isn't that fun and, well . . ."

Veronica rolls away from me into a squat. She grins. "Now, *that's* what I'm talking about," she says. "A perfect Heel Sweep. Did you guys see?" My friends look equal parts shocked and dismayed. "That's how it's done. That's how you protect yourself. Focus. Follow through. Success." I don't have the heart to explain that I had neither focus nor follow-through and the success was accidental.

Veronica scans the room. "Who's next?"

Chapter 30

ZACHARY'S RULES.

WE LIE IN A HEAP on the floor by the rickety table. Toby sits on a chair, tapping away on Monster Mayhem 2.0. He has enough points to buy one weapon to help take down the Hobgoblin.

"What do you guys think?" Toby asks. "Stun gun or ropes?"

When we respond with a series of groans, he eyes us skeptically. "Veronica wasn't so bad."

"That's because you were exempt," snarls Charlotte.

"*Someone* had to keep an eye on the phone." Toby sniffs.

"I would have volunteered to hold it," I say. "So, you know, you could practice your Heel Sweeps."

"No thanks," he says. "Besides, it's a spy school for *girls*, remember? Boys just provide support." For the first time, he looks positively gleeful at his exclusion from the club.

"It was awesome," Izumi moans. "I can't wait to do it again." Before we can ask the girl who was repeatedly flattened under Veronica's mean foot to explain, Toby's phone buzzes, and he tosses it up in the air like it's on fire.

"It's the map!" he hollers, even though we sit not two feet from him. Veronica flies into the room. She's wearing one of Angus's spy suits. Yes, it's true, I'm insanely jealous. It's black and gray with zippered pockets that I just know hide fantastic lifesaving, villain-incapacitating devices. And all we have are lame backpacks full of school supplies.

"It's the location," Toby says again, grabbing up the phone and turning the screen toward Veronica. We huddle around trying for a glimpse. An empty glowing cage hangs over the Tower of London, where two of Henry VII's wives, Anne Boleyn and Catherine Howard, were beheaded. This is not a comforting thought.

"How does this work?" Veronica asks quietly. "I've never played Monster Mayhem."

We gasp in horror. "Never?" asks Izumi. "As in, not even once?"

"Getting into spy college is not easy," Veronica barks.

"There's no time for trivial pursuits like video games."

"Nope," says Charlotte, "not even once."

"Will you guys shut up?" Toby pleads. "Listen, it's easy. This is the cage we need to put the monster in, once we find it. It's probably somewhere in the Tower, but the only way to know is to go there ourselves and search for it. Remember Monster Mayhem is about moving around in the world and seeing things. Right now my health is yellow. If it goes to red, then I go back to square one and can't hunt platinum monsters and we lose, so we need to keep an eye on that, too. If we capture five platinum monsters, we get Drexel back. Or that's what we've been told, anyway." Doubt clouds Toby's face. He wants to believe that he's playing Zachary's game on a level field, but we all know that's probably not the case.

"We'd better go," I say.

Out on the street, despite the urgency of our mission, Toby needs to stop for food. He buys fish and chips wrapped in greasy newspaper and makes happy noises all the way down to the edge of the River Thames, where we catch a river bus.

We don't have river buses in Connecticut. The low-slung ferry is blue and white with a bar and small café in the center. Despite the fact we are not on the typical tourist circuit, it's our first cool London outing and we're excited. Too excited for Veronica. She reminds us that we are not here for pleasure and that we should conduct ourselves with the seriousness appropriate to our situation. This cracks us up and Veronica goes to sit on the opposite side of the sleek river bus. She actually pretends she doesn't know us. The rain falls harder, and thick fog covers the city. A perfect day for sightseeing.

Before too long, to the left of the iconic Tower Bridge, we spy medieval fortifications looming in the heavy mist. Although it is now a museum, over the years the Tower of London has been a fortress, a palace, and a prison, depending on the needs of the reigning king. In the 1200s, it held a zoo of royal beasts—leopards, tigers, elephants, an ostrich, a bear—all given to the kings as gifts. So a Hobgoblin is no big deal, right? It's also a place where queens were beheaded and prisoners tortured and executed. Let's hope it doesn't come to that.

The river bus glides up to Tower Pier, and we climb off along with about a dozen other intrepid tourists. Toby is glued to his phone, waiting for more information, watching the countdown clock anxiously. Charlotte keeps an arm on him to make sure he doesn't trip and fall in the river. As we draw closer to the Tower, the Monster Mayhem map zooms in, giving us more details about the location of our Hobgoblin. We enter the Tower, where a Yeoman Warder dressed in an elaborate bright red costume, holding an umbrella, invites us to join his tour. He promises exciting tales from the Tower's grizzly past.

Izumi eyes him longingly. "Can we do it? There's so much history here, it's amazing!"

"No," Veronica says flatly. "Did you not hear the part when I told you we weren't sightseeing?"

"Yes," says Izumi. "But . . ."

Veronica narrows her gaze, and Izumi goes silent. We stand close to Toby, peering at the screen. "Where to?" Veronica asks.

Toby licks his lips and shifts uncomfortably. "The torture chamber," he says, holding up the phone. "The bottom of Wakefield Tower."

"You're kidding, right?" I ask.

"Nope."

"You guys," Charlotte says. "It's just a museum. Relax already." And while I understand this on a logical level, I still grab Izumi's hand and she doesn't shake me loose. Quickly, we walk between the exterior and interior fortified walls in the direction of the torture chamber. A murder of legendary Tower crows swoop down, squawking like maniacs and landing on the fortress walls. They watch us with beady eyes as we parade along beneath them. *Seriously? Crows?*

The entrance to the torture chamber is narrow. We head down stone steps to a wooden staircase within. Inside is oddly bright and cheery. The overhead lights illuminate exhibits featuring all the terrible ways the prisoners were worked over for information. There's a replica of the rack, which literally pulled a prisoner apart, and the Scavenger's Daughter, a diabolical contraption that did the exact opposite, crushing a person like a nut in a nutcracker. And if that's not enough, how about the manacles used to hang a prisoner by his arms for days on end?

"This is horrible," Charlotte says with distaste.

Veronica gives her a small smile. "And you'd think by now we'd know better."

Toby interrupts. "You guys, there's a Hobgoblin down here."

Chapter 31

DIDN'T ANNE BOLEYN DIE HERE?

WE ALL FRANTICALLY look around as if we might actually see a Hobgoblin bouncing around the torture chamber. Toby holds the phone out, sweeping it before him like he's combing the beach with a metal detector.

"It's under the rack," he whispers, climbing over the barrier to the exhibit. If anyone walks in now, we're going to British jail. Toby squats down and peers under the rack.

"Hello, little guy," he says. His fingers fly furiously across his screen. "Now just hold still. There you go. Gotcha!" He stands, triumphant, and knocks over a display case beside the rack. It crashes to the ground. He scrambles around the mess.

"Go!" Veronica commands, pointing to the stairs on the opposite side of the room. We sprint, thunderous footsteps of security close behind.

At the top of the stairs are a handful of tourists wandering around. At least three of them are playing Monster Mayhem, but not our sinister version. Casually, we cross the courtyard and huddle under an overhang, around Toby.

The Hobgoblin is not happy. The ugly little creature rattles the bars of his cage. He hisses and claws at us with sharp nails.

"Nice dude," Toby says. The creatures in Monster Mayhem 1.0 aren't quite as angry-looking. Many of them are cute, with bright colors and big eyes with long lashes. They purr and hum and blink at you. I don't remember any of them hissing.

Toby's health is solidly green, and he's earned a few points, although not nearly what he should for a platinum-level creature like the Hobgoblin. Zachary is a cheater on top of being a lunatic.

"Three down. Two to go," Charlotte says.

"This is a stupid game," Veronica says flatly.

I used to like Monster Mayhem. No. "Like" isn't the proper word. I was obsessed with it. I'd sit in math class and dream about which monsters I'd round up next and how they could help me to the next level. But now I'm leaning toward Veronica's assessment. Stupid.

We are traipsing toward the exit when suddenly Veronica jumps as if she's been stung by a bee. She pulls out her Center spy smartphone, the kind we are not allowed to have for reasons too annoying to believe, and groans. "It's Director Gladwell. You guys stay here and don't move. Got it?"

We agree, and she disappears across the quad, out of sight. Five minutes pass, and she doesn't come back. Gladwell must have heard about our protocol breaches, and now Veronica's being blamed. It's no wonder she doesn't like us.

Toby studies his screen, his brows knit together with concern.

"You guys?" He turns the phone toward us. It's full of brightly colored fireworks with streamers and balloons falling from the sky. The words *Bonus Round* fade in.

"Oh, no," Izumi yelps. As the screen resolves to a map, a red timer appears. It's counting down from twenty-five minutes. We all start screaming at once.

"We can win the game!"

"What's the creature?"

"Where is it?"

"Let's go! We're running out of time!"

The map pinpoints our bonus Ghoul right around the London Eye, the enormous Ferris wheel right on the banks of the River Thames, built to celebrate the millennium and kept on because everyone loves it. I've been to London a number of times, but the Eye never made it onto our itinerary. Who knew a visit would come as a result of a Monster Mayhem bonus round?

"I'll get Veronica!" I yell, sprinting across the courtyard. But I can't find her. I look everywhere. I race back to report her disappearance.

"We have to leave her," says Charlotte.

"She'll kill us," responds Izumi.

"It's for the mission," I say. "The mission comes first."

"Otherwise we fail," adds Toby. No one wants to fail. We bolt for the river bus.

On the ride, we try not to think about what happens the next time we see Veronica. Arguing that it was for the good of the mission is likely to get me heel-swept out with the trash. The countdown clock continues to march toward zero.

The giant white wheel comes into view, backed by Westminster Bridge, the Parliament building, and Big Ben. Our power is critically red. If we hurry, we might just make it. The river bus pulls to the dock, and we jump off before it's fully stopped. The captain howls at us, using some not-nice language, but we run down the ramp for the Eye, just next to the pier.

"Where's the Ghoul?" I yell.

"On the ride!"

Finally, a purpose for the rain and fog—no line.

"Hurry!"

We dash to the boarding point. Toby's eyes jump from reality to his screen and back again. Before we know it, we're swept into a huge glass capsule.

"Yes!" Toby pumps a fist into the air. "I got him! I got the Ghoul!" Relief floods me. We won the bonus round. We have five platinum creatures—a Quinotaur, a Snallygaster, a Goatman, a Hobgoblin, and a Ghoul. The game should be over! It's then I notice we're not alone in the capsule.

Seated on the bench in the corner is a boy I recognize. The only thing missing is the hat. He doesn't even look at us when he says, "Congratulations. And welcome."

Chapter 32

THE GAME CHANGES.

TOBY FREEZES. We have just locked ourselves in a tiny space with Zachary Hazard, evil Monster Mayhem master-mind. Where are our Center minders when we need them? They have to be tracking us. They have to be close.

"So the bad guy has us again?" Izumi asks. She doesn't sound angry or scared, just resigned. This makes me feel worse.

"Looks that way." Charlotte plops into a seat.

"Where's Drexel?" Toby demands.

Zachary waves him off. "Everyone is somewhere. But I've been thinking. While this game is superfun and I've enjoyed watching you struggle, I have a larger problem that needs fixing. I need you to hack the Center."

"What did you just say?"

"You heard me. Your beloved Center, that place you'd do anything for, even *betray* your friends."

I shiver. Zachary is going for the throat. Toby takes a few hard swallows. "What do you want from the Center?"

Zachary laughs. "The Black Book, of course."

"It doesn't exist," Toby says too quickly. "We looked for it, remember? It's just a rumor."

"I happen to know it isn't *just a rumor*. And you're going to get it for me."

"You're changing the rules of the game," Toby says, licking his lips. "We were playing for Drexel, not the Black Book."

"So what? Maybe I'm not giving you a choice. Just like you never gave *me* a choice."

"I did," Toby insists. "I asked you to stop. You wouldn't."

Zachary waves this off as an annoyance. "Whatever. It doesn't matter. In the end, you did me a favor. I'm having so much more fun now than when I was trapped in that horrible school."

"Revenge always backfires," Izumi offers.

Zachary glares at her. "Who asked you?"

"No one. I'm just saying. Seems like something you should know."

Slowly, we spin over the highest point on the eye. We are above Parliament and Big Ben, and the people down on the Queen's Walk look like ants.

"I won't hack the Center," Toby growls.

"Oh, but you will," Zachary replies. "If you want to save your friends, that is." With that, he grabs Toby's phone and smashes it against the metal frame of the capsule. It shatters into a million tiny shards.

The game is over. We go dark.

And the game is not the only thing that's over. Our London Eye ride is coming to an end, and we haven't taken even a moment to appreciate it. But it's hard to enjoy the scenery when your life is in danger.

"Let them go," Toby hisses. "This is about you and me."

"I didn't drag them into it," Zachary points out. "You did. I said at the beginning you were supposed to do this alone. But did you listen? No, you didn't. You Smith kids think you can get away with anything."

I clear my throat. "We're a team. And we stick together."

"Yeah," says Charlotte. "And we're a pretty good one, present situation excepted."

"A team?" Zachary says with a sneer. His eyes are bright

and wild and his cheeks flushed. "How nice for you. But in reality, teams are just stupid and never get anything done. Teams are weak."

"So what are you saying exactly?" I ask.

"Abby, be quiet," Toby whispers. His face is shiny with sweat. Zachary gets right in my personal space. I can't back away because there's nowhere to go.

"Who *are* you?" he asks.

"No one," I say.

Our capsule slides into the docking bay, where we're meant to exit by jumping out as the capsule slows down. I mentally relay a message to my friends: *When the door opens, run.* I'm pretty sure Izumi gets it. As for the others, who knows?

"Here's how this is going to work," Zachary says. "I have a car waiting that will take us to a secret location where you will do what I ask. If you're successful and well behaved, you'll get to leave with your friends and Drexel. If not, well, then I can't really say what will happen."

Izumi puts herself right in front of the door. Zachary doesn't notice. She squares her shoulders just like she does in rugby, ready to take out any obstacles in her path. Charlotte stands close to me. Her knees are slightly bent. We're in ready position.

Zachary is not much bigger than me. Anything he throws we should be able to take. Sure, I'm not factoring in his first-class ticket on the crazy train, but I'd hate to fail on our very first mission at the hands of a peer. That seems especially lame. The door swings open, and the friendly attendants invite us to exit.

"Don't make any sudden moves," Zachary advises. "Do you see those guys, the ones in the black coats? Those are my people. They're going to escort us to the car. If you try to escape, they'll catch you, so it's pointless. I only get the best when it comes to personal security. It's important in today's world."

I really don't like Zachary. Who does he think he is anyway? I study the men in black winter coats. There are three of them, broad-shouldered with perfectly combed hair. They wear blank expressions as they move closer. Despite the muscle, we still have to run. Izumi gets down low. She plows into the leading black-coated guy, taking him out at the knees. This gives us the chance to scatter. We break in four different directions. I run toward a kiosk selling tickets to kitschy London tourist attractions and sprint down the Queen's Way toward Westminster Bridge. My breath comes in hard, fast gasps. The cold air sears my lungs. I lose myself in a crowd waiting to enter the London Dungeon and finally slow to a walk.

When the escape plan is "scatter," it usually comes with a second part about where to meet up after you've evaded the bad guys. Unfortunately, we never got to that stage of planning.

I cut back on the sidewalk, throwing quick glances over my shoulder. No sign of any black-coated men. But no sign of my friends either. I'm back where we started, near the river bus pier. And it's from there that I see the back of Charlotte's jacket as she's shoved into the big SUV. I frantically scan the crowd. Only strangers. Is it possible that I'm the only one who got away? My chest feels tight. I bend over and try to calm my breath. A lady with a nice face asks me if I'm okay. I am definitely not okay. I have no way to find my friends. They have disappeared.

A river bus pulls up and I hop on, huddled against the window, watching the rain fall down. If this is about torturing Toby and extracting revenge for something that happened a few years ago, what does Zachary want with the Black Book? Is it just another way to hurt Toby?

As the boat cuts through the water, I have an awful thought, a possible intersection between the Black Book and Monster Mayhem 2.0. Zachary already has control of the game. He can roll it out to the millions and millions of users at any time. Through the game, he can make them do whatever he wants. He can walk them right off cliffs if he feels like it, without anyone ever looking up.

I wrap my arms around myself, suddenly chilled to the bone. And maybe the only thing standing between Zachary and total mind control of all these players are the Center agents. If he can neutralize the agents, he's free to do as he pleases.

A million terrible scenarios run through my head. He can create an instant mob with a rare monster worth lots of points, and he can do this anywhere on the map. He can initiate battles between players that quickly spill over from virtual reality to the actual streets. He can control the ebb and flow of people everywhere.

One thing is clear. I need to rescue my team, and to do that I need dry clothes, a snack, and my pink backpack. As the river bus gently pulls to my stop, I make a plan. First, I find out where Zachary took them. Then I go there. And I free them. All before Toby is forced to hack the Center. Easy.

Except it never is.

Chapter 33

GOING ROGUE IS NOT AS GLAMOROUS AS IT SOUNDS.

I POUND ON THE DOOR of the safe house, fully expecting a furious Veronica to answer the door. But after a minute this looks unlikely, and people are starting to stare. As casually as possible, I pick the lock. For a safe house, it's not very safe.

Inside, there is no sign of Veronica. There's no one else from the Center either. The next time they send me on a mission and promise to be watching the whole time, ready to intervene at a moment's notice, I'm going to call foul. My stomach growls as I climb the stairs like an old lady. The jet lag makes my eyelids heavy and crusty. I could call my mother and tell her what's going on. I could call Director

Gladwell. But inevitably they will tell me to wait for a team to arrive, to do nothing. And I don't have time to wait. I have to go after my friends, and I have to do it now.

I pull my pink backpack from the pile on the floor, but before heading back downstairs I make a pit stop in Veronica's room. A silver suitcase sits on top of her bed. It's open, revealing a neatly folded extra Angus suit. I pull it out and give it a shake. It unfurls with a snap. I run my fingers down the sleek fabric, and before I can talk myself out of it, I'm trying it on. It fits perfectly. I slide on the black boots. They're a little wide but wearable. I admire my reflection in the mirror attached to the back of the bedroom door. I look amazing! Intimidating! Smart! Scary!

Who am I kidding? I look like an unemployed superhero trying too hard to be cool. But the suit is the ultimate in cargo pants, with dozens of secret pockets, so even if I do look like a dork I'm wearing it. Plus, it's waterproof. I grab my backpack and descend on the kitchen. I make a quick peanut butter sandwich, but I have a hard time swallowing. I discard the sandwich and shovel in a few chocolate cookies, washed down with cold tea leftover from this morning.

The sugar helps me think more clearly. I empty the backpack contents on the kitchen table and begin to dig.

The first thing I need to do is find where Zachary took them. I locate the tracker card and almost scream when it's got zero charge. Didn't Angus say it never needed charging? Wasn't that the point of the old-school-is-better lecture? Oh, I miss my rhinestone Abby phone!

I eat some more cookies while the tracker juices up, thinking about how many times spies are thwarted because of dead electronics. It's amazing we can ever get anything done. By the time the tube of cookies is gone, the tracker is ready to roll. I turn it on, and it happily blinks and beeps, indicating Izumi, Toby, and I are all here in the house.

My heart sinks as I race for the backpacks, dumping their contents on the floor. And there with the other school supplies are the tracking wristbands. I want to cry. By the time we find them, it will be too late. But in my hand the tracker starts to flash.

Charlotte!

She had the bracelet wrapped up in her mop of hair! No *guy* is going to notice that. A string of numbers appears on the screen. I press the button, and an address replaces the geographical coordinates. I got them! I don't have a real map, so I can't actually see where they are relative to me, but the name of the town sounds vaguely familiar. East Molesey. I know that's a train stop.

My pockets bulge with the contents of my backpack, but the people headed in and out of the Underground pay me no attention. Something sharp stabs me in the back as I try to get comfortable in my seat. I hope whatever it is doesn't accidentally electrocute me.

The train chugs along. I sit back and chew my cuticles. When I'm done, I bite my nails. Passengers get on and off. One stop at a time, we move closer to my destination. By the time the train pulls into the Hampton Court stop, I'm a nervous wreck. This is no way to start a rescue. Outside the window, I can just see the top of the Hampton Court Palace walls. Can't spit in this place without hitting a palace.

I disembark and ask five different people before I find one who recognizes the address I seek.

"That old place?" the man asks. "What do you want with it?"

"I'm a photographer doing a project for school," I say, smiling enthusiastically. The guy buys it, and twenty minutes later, I stand outside a decrepit mansion. And it just had to be creepy. It couldn't be a nice, modern mansion. Rain drips off the ends of my hair, but the rest of me is dry. I'm keeping this suit. I don't care what anyone says.

I approach the heavy iron gate, fronting a twisty driveway leading to the house. When I was little, Jennifer used to tell me that being afraid was good because fear let you know when you should be alert and aware. She said it was the body's way of turning on all the lights and getting ready. I'm afraid now, but it doesn't feel useful. It feels like something I need to overcome if I'm going to take the first step down this long driveway. It's just one foot in front of the other. Now go.

All goes well for about sixty seconds, when I discover the ornate iron gates are padlocked. The stone pillars to either side are impossible to scale, and the surrounding fence is topped with razor wire. There are also security cameras. Doesn't anyone in this neighborhood find it strange that an abandoned house is protected by state-of-the-art security? Hiding in the shadows, I dig through my pockets until I find the communications disruptor bookmark. I can't remember if Angus said it worked on security cameras, but I shall soon find out. Flipping it on, I prop it against a concrete pillar. It glows a dark red that I hope means it's busy interrupting.

Next I pull out the nail file kit. But this is no baby safe house lock. This is a padlock that is not going to yield to my amateur skills. A setback, yes, but good spies rally and find a workaround. I pull out the ChapStick, turn the cap counterclockwise, wedge it beside the lock, and leap behind a row of hedges.

With a loud *pop*, the lock explodes and bits of shrapnel go flying everywhere. I wait to see if anyone comes out to check on the commotion, but no one does, which can only mean the bookmark works! Mad scientist Angus is my new favorite person! I hope I live long enough to tell him. The gates creak open. Weeds burst through cracks in the driveway's fractured pavement. I stay in the shadows.

This suit definitely makes me faster. And helps me blend in. There are several black SUVs parked along the driveway. I drop some Life Savers in each tank. Now no one can escape. This is kind of fun.

The mansion comes into view. It's enormous, with turrets on both ends and sharp peaked roofs in between. The red brick is dirty from neglect. A tangle of brambles consumes the path leading to the front entrance. The windows are thick with grime. Somewhere, an owl hoots mournfully.

I steel myself. My friends are in this horrible place, and I need to get them out. A shadow passes one of the first-floor windows, and I jump behind a crop of weeds. There is no way this falling-down old wreck of a building is 100 percent secure. There has to be a way in.

Staying low, I creep around the perimeter. The brambles

tangle in my hair and catch my suit, and each time I think it's hands grabbing me. I focus on counting backward from one hundred. This is all going to be fine. I'm going to get in here, get my friends, and get out. And no one will catch me.

"Looky, looky. What have we here?"

Well, maybe it's not going to happen exactly like that. One of the black-coated men from the London Eye looms large. He holds a wooden baton in one hand and slaps the palm of his other hand with it expectantly.

"The one that got away," Baton Boy says with a sinister smile. Hey, I kind of like that better than "the headmaster's daughter," which is how people usually refer to me. "But then was stupid enough to come back. Did you really think you were going to get in here and free your pals?"

"Yes?" I imagine I don't look very intimidating with plant life stuck in my hair. I straighten up to my full height, and I still only come up to Baton Boy's shoulder. The rhythm of his slapping grows faster. He'd really like an excuse to use that baton on me. But I have a different idea.

Awkwardly wedged in my pocket is the can of Pringles. When I move to pull it out, Baton Boy freaks, waving his stick around like a lunatic. "Hands where I can see them! I'm not fooled just because you're a kid!"

"Relax," I say. "I'm starving. It's been a long day." I peel the lid off the can and offer it up. "You want some?"

Pringles are irresistible. Everyone knows that. The baton pauses in midair. "I guess so," he says. I toggle the switch with my thumb.

When he reaches out, I heave the can at his boots, and instantly he's encased in thick, hard goop up to his calves. He lunges at me, but I'm light on my feet, as Owen Elliott suggested, and I dodge his baton. He falls over backward as the paralytic begins to work, and within seconds he can't move. His lips flap like a fish out of water.

"It's not permanent," I say. "Be good and I'll come back with the antidote." I can't, of course, because I don't have the antidote, but he doesn't need to know that. Abby: 1, Bad Guys: 0. I take off around the base of the house. It's time for me to get inside this place.

Chapter 34

BREAKING AND ENTERING.

AROUND THE BACK, I find a narrow ground-level window that looks like it drops into a stone cellar. If I make myself really small, I might be able to squeeze through. I estimate it's about six feet to the ground. That's not too bad. I can handle six feet.

I pull the sleeve of my spy suit down over my fist and punch in the windowpane. It shatters, leaving behind bits of glass, like sharks' teeth, protruding from the frame. As I peer through, I imagine a time when this mansion was grand and the cellar was full of expensive wine and smelly wheels of cheese.

I crunch into a tight ball and wiggle awkwardly

through. With a final push, I fall ten feet with a *thud*. So much for eyeballing the distance to the ground. But I hear the faintest hiss, and the suit inflates just enough to cushion me. I'm dressed in an airbag! A second later, the puffiness disappears, and I'm shoulder to shoulder with the cold stone floor. The cellar stinks of mold and decay. The rain has eaten away the plaster walls, and the supporting timbers are rotted. The only light is the very pale excuse for daytime outside the broken windows.

I get to my feet and dust off.

All is quiet. I take the mostly collapsed stairs out of the cellar. I fall through on the fourth one, making such a racket I'm sure I'm busted. But nothing happens. I pull myself up and cautiously climb to the top.

The door, long gone, opens to a wide servants' kitchen. Most everything has been scavenged over the years. All that remains is a table with three legs and some broken pieces of pottery. Dust and cobwebs cover every surface. A thick green vine crawls from the cracked window up the wall. I walk gingerly across uneven stones and out the other side into a hallway, which spits me out into an imposing foyer. The skeleton of what once was a grand chandelier hangs from fraying wires. A grand staircase sweeps upward, with an ornately carved banister just barely hanging on.

I climb quickly. At the top, I stumble over an abandoned pair of old shoes and a tarnished silver hairbrush. A rustling from one of the rooms stops me dead in my tracks. I slip behind a door hanging from its hinges, flatten against the wall, and try not to breathe.

From my position, I can see an old-fashioned sitting room fronting another room with its door closed. In the sitting room are two more of the bad guys, coats removed. One has huge feet propped up on a desk holding a bank of monitors. The other has a big red nose that he dabs with a hanky. All the monitors carry images of fuzz. My bookmark disruptor is doing its thing! Big Foot and Red Nose argue.

"This is your fault," says Big Foot. They push buttons and rotate knobs with obvious frustration.

"Don't blame me," says Red Nose. "You're the one who messed up the whole system."

"Did not!"

"What are you, five years old?"

Big Foot waves him off. "When do we rotate out of here, anyway?" he asks. "This is boring. I like it better in the dungeon."

"It's not a dungeon," says Red Nose. "It's an interrogation facility. You should pay closer attention."

There's a pause during which Big Foot loses his train of

thought. "I'm hungry," he says finally. "When's dinner?" Red Nose rolls his eyes. I'd feel almost sorry for him if he weren't a bad guy. A team is only as strong as its weakest link.

I roll back on my heels. So I guess I have to know what's behind that door. About ten feet down the hallway is an elaborate skylight in the shape of a dome with two intact glass panels remaining. If I can break the panels, Red Nose and Big Foot will run out to investigate, and I'll run in. I do a mental inventory of my pockets. What will smash glass? Nothing. Why don't I have spare exploding ChapSticks? Or even a tennis ball? But spies are supposed to think out of the box. What can I throw to break the glass panels?

As quietly as I can, I expand the water bottle and stuff in the night-vision sunglasses to give the bottle some heft. But it's not enough. There's no way I can get this bottle to fly ten feet and hit the glass. I glue the nail polish bottle to the bottom of the bottle, along with my thumb. I detach myself, leaving behind a layer of skin for my effort. My contraption looks like a satellite that had a run-in with Dr. Frankenstein. But it doesn't need to be pretty to get the job done.

Like the stealthy ninja warrior I am in my dreams, I creep closer to the door and hunker down. I have a lot of doubts, like if this doesn't work I'm toast, but before those doubts paralyze me, I fling the water bottle at the skylight with all of my might.

The bottle hits the glass dead center, and the glass explodes. Big Foot and Red Nose leap to their feet and rush into the hallway. I slip into the room and quickly enter the closed room, shutting the door behind me.

And there is *Veronica*.

Veronica? What is she doing here? She's tied to a chair with a gag in her mouth. Her eyes register surprise, followed by fury that may not be directed entirely at me. Quickly, I drop to my knees and cut her loose with the Swiss Army Knife. She pulls the gag from her mouth and holds a finger to her lips for silence. Which is probably a good thing because I was just about to gloat about how this is the second time I've saved her life, even if I haven't actually saved anything yet.

Outside the door, there is grumbling. "Birds," Red Nose suggests.

"You think?" asks Big Foot.

"You got a better idea?"

"Nope."

"Didn't think so."

"You gonna report it?"

Red Nose's eyes go wide. "No way. The less I interact with that crazy kid, the better."

"Agreed."

I assume they've settled back into their seats to stare at the fuzzy monitors. Using hand signals, Veronica asks how many are outside the door. I hold up two fingers. I try to mime that they are sitting at a table, but Veronica looks at me like I'm insane. Then she does some more hand signals that I think are meant to explain her plan, but I don't get any of it and I'm not sure how to say I don't understand in made-up sign language. Turns out it doesn't matter because we're on the move. Veronica crouches low by the door and indicates I should do the same on the other side. Gently, she turns the knob and pushes the door open just a crack. When it is about a foot open, they notice.

"Hey, what do you think you're doing, missy?" Big Foot snarls, striding toward the door. "How'd you get out of—" Veronica pulls the door back and slams it full force into Big Foot's face. He drops like a rag doll. That was excellent! I need to remember that one.

What happens next is so fast, when it's over all I know is that Red Nose is tied to his seat, head lolling like his neck no longer works, with Veronica's gag in his mouth.

"Incompetent fools," she says, and turns her attention to me. "*What* are you doing here?"

"Rescuing you guys?"

Her eyes narrow. "You *guys*? I told you at the Tower not to move. Have you ever met an order you were willing to follow?" I hang my head. Veronica is disappointed in me again. There is no point in offering excuses, even if I have many, starting with where did she go and where was the backup and why does this *always* happen? "Now tell me everything. All the details."

I start from the moment we were separated at the Tower and bring her right up to the windows. She's not happy about Toby and the part about hacking the Black Book.

"Who does this little brat think he is?" she growls.

I don't know the answer to that, but he's doing a good job messing things up so far. More important, she's not impressed by how I used the Pringles. This bums me out. I consider it some of my best work.

Veronica paces in front of the tied-up men. "So you didn't see anyone else in the house?"

"No," I say. "But these guys were talking about some sort of dungeon interrogation place."

"That must be where they are. Hey, did you steal that suit from my suitcase?"

A prickly flush rises on my cheeks. "Yes."

"It looks good on you," she says after a pause. "Come on. Let's find this dungeon."

Two things have happened. The first is Veronica has taken over my mission. She is now clearly in charge. The second is that I'm relieved. I hurry after her, not the least bit interested in being left behind.

Chapter 35

IT'S REALLY BAD WHEN IT'S WORSE THAN I THOUGHT.

ON THE FIRST FLOOR in a hallway is a door that does not fit the rest of the ramshackle mansion. It's brand-new and made of heavy steel. Suddenly, Veronica is patting me down like I'm a suspect in a crime.

"Hey!"

"I need the lock-picking kit," she says. "It's in here somewhere."

"Actually, I think I left it on the driveway." I know I did. Right before I blew up the padlock.

"Then give me your pen," she says. "You have the pen, don't you?"

I dutifully hand over the acid-filled pen. Veronica shoves

it in the lock and hits the button. The lock begins to hiss and steam and melt. We open the door to reveal a stairway leading down into darkness. We creep about halfway down the concrete stairs when Veronica holds up a hand for me to stop. At the bottom of the stairs sit two new guards in black suits. They're multiplying like weeds. These two wave their phones around looking for a signal, complaining they don't work. I smile smugly even if no one can see me.

Veronica lays out our plan in sign language. Once again, I have no idea what I'm supposed to do, but I nod enthusiastically. A good spy sometimes just has to wing it. Suddenly, Zachary emerges from the dark side of the room.

"How's it going, boss?" asks a guard.

"Not as fast as I'd like," Zachary says, annoyed. He kicks open a small refrigerator packed with Coke and chugs a full can in a single gulp. How does he not explode? After a giant burp, he says, "You'd think he'd be motivated."

Veronica flashes me a look. That doesn't sound good. Zachary grabs an extra soda and stalks off, out of sight. My palms are slick. We're sneaking up on two armed men in a tight space with a single escape route. How come Veronica is smiling? It's possible she thinks this is fun.

And *I* think my job is to be an observer, as in I observe Veronica creep up behind the two guards and smack their heads together. It makes a sickening sound like a dropped watermelon. One slumps over immediately, but the other reaches back and grabs Veronica. He gets a hand around her knee and squeezes so hard I see the white bone of his knuckles through his skin. Veronica's face scrunches in pain. She brings the elbow of her left arm directly down on the top of his skull. That does the trick. The guy topples off the couch and onto the floor. She takes a second to glare at him before collapsing to one knee. Her face is ghostly pale.

I rush to her side and prop her up against me. "I can't walk," she says. This is so not what I want to hear. Her knee is already a funny shade of purple.

"I can help you."

"No," she says sternly. "You have to find the others. Time is critical. If Zachary gets the Black Book, the Center is compromised and a lot of people will be in danger. We can't let that happen."

Veronica sees the fear on my face.

"Abby. You can do this. Listen, the reason I give you such a hard time is because I want you to be better. I want you always to be pushing the limits. Do you understand?"

"So you're mean to me because you like me?" I ask.

"Yes. Sort of. This mission is up to you. And I know you can get it done. Now go."

Am I glowing? I feel like I'm glowing. But I should stop glowing because that is no way to sneak up on someone in a dark place. I tuck Veronica out of sight behind an old sofa and promise I'll be back.

"Good luck," she whispers.

My mouth is so dry I can't answer. I head into the darkness where Zachary disappeared. It's a low-slung tunnel that reminds me of the entrance to the Catacombs. The ground is rough and bumpy, and I stumble several times, but I don't dare use a flashlight.

After what seems like forever, the wide mouth of the tunnel comes into view, revealing an enormous underground cavern. It is definitely movie-set quality and so cold I can see my breath. Off to the right is a long table with a bunch of computers. In front of the computers sits Toby, his shoulders hunched, head down. Zachary paces behind him.

But that's not the best part. No, the best part would be the cage suspended over a smooth concrete tank filled with water. In the cage are Izumi, Charlotte, and Drexel Caine, hands bound behind their backs, gags in their mouths, huddled together for warmth. I flatten against the tunnel wall, my heart racing. Veronica said I could do this. She said the reason she's tough on me is because I'm good. Right? While I'm contemplating my relationship with Veronica, the cage gives a sudden lurch and drops about three feet. It now dangles just over the water.

Zachary laughs maniacally, waving around the remote that controls the cage. Toby reacts poorly to this, lunging for Zachary, who drops the cage another two feet.

"Remember the water is zero degrees," Zachary says with a wicked smile. "Or for you American types, thirty-two degrees Fahrenheit. Once your father and friends submerge, they will die in about fifteen minutes. You better hurry up."

"I'm doing the best I can," Toby barks.

"Are you? I'd have thought you'd be through by now. You're supposed to be such an excellent hacker. Maybe that's all talk."

Toby's face collapses. "I'm trying," he mutters. "I'm close. I really am."

And he really is. He'd hack the Black Book, the heart and soul of the Center, to save Drexel, Izumi, and Charlotte. Suddenly, I'm filled with warmth. Toby really is part of our team. But it's a good thing I'm here. Because there is no way I'm going to let him down and make him do what Zachary is asking. Despite what happened with *Mona Lisa*, we really are in this together.

He's my friend.

Chapter 36

PLANS. WHY DON'T THEY EVER WORK FOR ME?

IN MY HEAD, the plan is flawless. I get Zachary's attention. He steps away from Toby. I hit him with the electrocuting pencil and he goes down. Toby grabs the remote and raises the cage and we save the world. See? Brilliant. Of course, most of my plans go awry as soon as they encounter reality.

I step out of the shadows. "Hi, Zachary," I say, casual even as my heart pounds ferociously in my chest. Zachary is surprised, although he pretends otherwise. All eyes in the cage turn to me.

"Abby Hunter." Zachary smirks. "The girl who will

never be as good as her mom." I guess he looked me up. Should I be flattered? No.

"Is that supposed to hurt my feelings?" My fingers rest lightly on my thigh, just grazing the tip of the pencil. I can't remember how to turn it on. *Great.*

"Yes! I want to hurt your feelings. And theirs!" He points to the cage. "But mostly I want to hurt Toby because Toby hurt me. We were best friends. He was supposed to have my back, but he betrayed me." I remember the bitter look on Zachary's face in the Paris hotel as he watched Toby with the other boys. It was the pain of believing your best friend would hurt you on purpose. What he doesn't see is how Toby was trying to save him.

"To have friends you first have to be a good friend," I say, moving closer. I need to be a pencil length from him for this to work. So maybe my plan isn't flawless, but my only other option was to hit him over the head with a flashlight, and that didn't seem any more promising. "And sometimes when your friends are acting weird, you have to forgive them. When they do things you don't understand, you have to ask them why. You don't just go immediately to kidnapping their dads."

"I *was* a good friend," Zachary insists. He takes a few steps toward me.

"No, you weren't. For example, you changed the rules of the game. You said if Toby caught the monsters he'd get his dad back. And now look at this! You lied. Friends don't lie."

Zachary's face goes beet red. He's so mad he's going to drop everyone in the freezing water just to have the last word. I clamp my lips shut before I do any more damage. Holding the remote in front of him, Zachary insists Toby zip-tie my hands behind my back. Now I'm in trouble.

As Toby finishes, he gives me a spontaneous hug. "Oh, Abby," he cries, "thank you for coming for us. You're a true friend. I'd be lost without you!"

This is so out of the ordinary for Toby that I almost ask him if he's ill. Good thing I don't.

"You're on," Toby whispers as Zachary screams for him to get back to work. He drops the cage another few inches just to make sure we remember who's in charge.

I'm on, as in Toby activated the pencil. It works by pressure, so all I have to do is get right up close to Zachary and bump him with my hip. Of course, this also means I get the shock. But I can handle it. I've handled it before. I clear my throat.

"Hey, Toby?"

"Be quiet, or you go in the cage too," growls Zachary.

I ignore him. "Toby, how about no rhinestones on my

next spy phone? I mean, I like it, but I'm not that girly, you know? Maybe just make it blue or something?"

"I said be quiet!"

"Or yellow. I really like yellow. It's such a happy color. Like sunflowers. What do you think?"

As Zachary closes the distance between us, I rush him. The Heel Sweep works perfectly. Zachary hits the ground. The remote bounces from his hand. Toby lunges for it at the same moment Zachary pulls me down. Struggling, I push my hip into his chest and we both convulse from the shock. But Zachary's not going down without a fight. He wraps his arms around me and we roll, the electricity pulsing through us, right over the lip of the concrete tank and into the freezing water.

In the split second before I hit the water, I wonder what Angus meant by "messy." I guess I'm going to find out. But at least my friends will get away, so it's worth it. It really is.

Everything goes black.

Chapter 37

IN TROUBLE. AGAIN.

CHARLOTTE, IZUMI, AND I stand against a wall outside the headmaster's office. It's been ten days since I took a swim with Zachary Hazard. We don't speak as we wait for the door to open. Soon, it does and Toby emerges, trailed by Drexel Caine. Drexel's back in an ill-fitting suit, but his shoulders sag as if he has suddenly realized the world can be a dangerous place.

Toby offers us a half smile. Drexel grabs my hands with his. They're cold, and I shiver. I don't know if I will ever be warm again.

"I want to thank you," Drexel says, his voice full of emotion. "For saving me, for saving *us*, and for giving me a second chance to be a better father." I throw Toby a glance. He rolls his eyes. Parents deciding to be "better" is a code-red emergency. It usually means increased supervision. Drexel will not let Toby out of his sight. Things are bad.

"I want you to know," Drexel continues, "that I'm shutting down Monster Mayhem for good. And you're to thank for that."

And they just got worse. I'm going to be the most hated person in the universe. "It wasn't all me," I say quickly. "It takes a team." Before Drexel can wreak further havoc on my reputation, the headmaster appears in the doorway.

"Ladies," she says. Drexel releases my hands. Toby mouths, *Good luck!* and we enter the inner sanctum. I swear the Tower of London felt more welcoming.

Jennifer wears an unreadable expression, which does not bode well for us. After Zachary and I tumbled into the concrete tank, Toby freed his dad and the girls and they fished me out. The doctor says I'm lucky to be alive because falling in the water with the spy pencil is the same as dropping a hair dryer in a bathtub. She says I'm tough as nails to survive it. Turns out Zachary Hazard is tough as nails too and is recovering in a secret location where he will no longer be a threat to society. It's interesting that no one will tell me where.

I want some sympathy for being electrocuted and drowned. I mean, my hair is literally fried. But sympathy will not be forthcoming. We may have saved the world, but that does not mean we aren't in trouble.

"First, you left school grounds without permission," says Jennifer. "Second, you bribed a ride to the airport with an individual not authorized to transport students. Third, you stole a plane. A plane! I can't believe I'm even saying that. Shall I continue? Why, yes, I shall! You failed to report the circumstances under which you were party to a violation of international law, specifically pulling an alarm in the *Mona Lisa* room."

"But . . . ," I interrupt.

She holds up a hand for silence. "Do not even try to defend your actions and choices. That will only make things worse. Moving on. You exchanged information with a notorious hacker named Iceman, potentially compromising the position of the Center on this same notorious hacker."

"Izzie's not that bad," mutters Charlotte.

"Excuse me?"

"Never mind."

"You failed to carry out specific orders in London, jeopardizing yourselves and others in the process. You ignored a directive from a Center director. In case you're wondering, that's not a good thing. And then you went and almost got yourself electrocuted! To summarize, you did everything wrong. Every. Single. Thing."

"But what were we supposed to do?" I blurt. "Veronica was kidnapped. Zachary compromised the Center's communications network so you guys thought we were at Buckingham Palace! We had no choice but to act!"

The minute the words leave my mouth, I regret them. All Jennifer sees is that we didn't do what we were supposed to do. A heavy silence fills the air. For the first time since arriving at Smith, I feel like my tenure here might be coming to an end. There's an uncomfortable flutter in my chest. Can Jennifer ground me until I'm thirty-five? Does a million demerits mean automatic expulsion? Did we finally go too far?

Jennifer looms over us. "However," she says slowly. A "however"! This is good. This means we still have hope. "You did manage to catch Zachary Hazard at great personal risk to yourself. And the importance of that is not lost on the Center. They appreciate that Hazard is no longer an active threat even if they are not completely comfortable with the way it happened. Therefore, your punishment for these many transgressions has been left to Smith to determine."

My mother would not kick me out of her own school, would she? I think about the time I found Veronica in the mansion and how happy I was to see her and how completely confident I was in her ability to get the job done.

In that moment, I know that however much I want to be a spy, I'm not ready. I need a lot of work. "I know we messed up," I say, contrite. "But we learned a lesson. We're not ready. Not yet." But we will be. We *will* be.

Jennifer doesn't respond. She fiddles with her Smith School lapel pin, removing it and placing it gently on the big tidy desk. It's actually so tidy as to be empty. No piles of paper, no framed photos of smiling Smith students, no paper clip jar or rubber bands. Even her coffee cup is missing. What's going on here?

Suddenly, the door to the office swings open and a familiar face walks in. As Jennifer steps out from behind the massive desk, I now understand why all of her stuff is gone. I know what's happening.

Mrs. Smith is *back.*

Acknowledgments

Writing a book takes a village, even if I do spend most of the time alone in that village, with just the weird people living in my head for company. Thank you to my agent extraordinaire, Leigh Feldman, and her remarkable assistant, Eliza Kirby. You guys are the best. And to my editor, Alyson Heller, a big thank-you for sticking with Abby and me through *Power Play*. Your enthusiasm and support smooth out the rough parts. And to the entire team at Aladdin, thank you for making the engine run. It would be lonely out here without you.

A big thanks to my 2017 Debut group. What a talented collection of writers! I've so enjoyed our journey through the middle-grade trenches. You've made it fun. To Chris Grabenstein and Wendelin Van Draanen for sharing your wit and wisdom with me—I'm ever grateful. And to Eileen Rendahl, my one-woman local writers' support group, thank you for understanding what I'm talking about without all the backstory.

And to Max and Katie, thank you for being funny and

curious and willing to hike to the top of Nevada Falls, even if the promised reward is the very dubious category of "scenery." You make me want to save the world. And finally, this book is for Mike, as they all are. Steady on.

**DON'T MISS
ABBY'S NEXT ADVENTURE!**

Double Cross

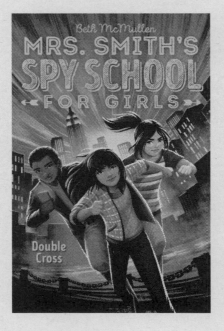

Chapter 1

SAVING THE WORLD IS NO EXCUSE.

IF YOU WANT TO BE A SPY, and possibly save the world, you have to practice. Take advantage of every opportunity to improve your skills. Me and my best friends, Charlotte and Izumi, are serious about spying, which is why we've spent the last month of summer on the Smith School for Children campus perfecting a karate move we call Deadhead the Rose, where we roundhouse kick the withered flowers from their stems to make way for new blooms. As a gardening technique, it is much faster than pruning shears. We've gotten pretty good. I can deadhead an entire rosebush in under a minute.

We're kicking roses outside Headmaster Smith's office

window, in New England heat so unrelenting Charlotte keeps pretending to faint just to get a break, when Izumi whispers, "You guys. Come here."

We peel off our gardening gloves and squeeze in tight next to Izumi under the window, wide-open in hopes of catching a passing breeze. The air is a thick, humid blanket we cannot throw off. Staying low, we peer over the window ledge. Inside, Mrs. Smith alternately studies a piece of paper and fans herself with it. These original Smith School buildings have no air conditioning. Global warming is now in a race with tradition to see who breaks first. Mrs. Smith wears a headset and her resting expression, which is total annoyance.

"It's not without precedent," she says into the headset. "I started with the spy school well before sixteen, as did others. If I want to let this girl in early, I'll do it. She could be our next Veronica Brooks. She has a brilliant mind. We don't want to lose students who are truly *exceptional*."

Everyone knows Veronica Brooks is the gold standard in spying, but who is the other girl Mrs. Smith is talking about? There's a pause in the conversation. Izumi elbows me, eyes wide.

"I'm not *asking* you," Mrs. Smith continues. "I'm *informing* you. As a courtesy. Now, you have a lovely day."

She tosses the headset on her desk in a way that leaves

the *lovely day* sentiment in doubt. We crawl away from the window on our hands and knees, to a safe distance, and all begin talking at once.

"Is it us?" I whisper. *Me? Is she finally going to let me into the spy school?*

Before this gets really confusing, an explanation. The Smith School for Children is exactly as it sounds: a preppy paradise of redbrick buildings, climbing ivy and students in uncomfortable uniforms. We have a Latin school motto, which loosely translates to "don't be a jerk," and a coat of arms featuring a roaring lion (not kidding). Our hallways are lined with portraits of former headmasters, none of whom look like they can take a joke.

But get closer. Go deeper. Look underneath the school. And I don't mean that metaphorically. Below the buildings in the old tunnels and passageways, the Center hides the spy school, a secret training facility for teenage girl spies, kids who are innocent-looking on the outside but sharp on the inside. These are the girls getting done what the adults cannot. Because, after all, who suspects a kid? Unless we are noisy or badly behaved, we are invisible. We can move through the world without warranting so much as a second glance. By the time you realize the Center spies have come for you, it's too late.

Mrs. Smith was a founding member of the spy school. As was my mother, Jennifer Hunter. Yes. My mother was a spy. *Is* a spy? Being as I didn't find out until I was twelve, and then only by accident, I'm still a bit fuzzy on the details. Right now I could not tell you where Jennifer is or what she is doing. At home in our tiny New York City apartment reading the latest Stephen King or apprehending a notorious arms smuggler in Yemen? Your guess is as good as mine. A proper teenager would rebel against all this spy nonsense and possibly choose a life of crime just to spite her spy mom. But I'm not ordinary. I want in on the spy gig. Badly.

Alas, spying is only for those sixteen and older, which means too bad for me, despite having saved the world *twice* on behalf of the Center. But this new evidence suggests that Mrs. Smith might have changed her mind about the age limit.

"We need to get in that office," says Charlotte. "As in right now."

Izumi puts her hand on Charlotte's shoulder. "Is this a good idea?" she asks. "I mean, the whole reason we're here working the grounds during vacation is because we're being punished. Remember?"

Oh. Right. True. A few months ago, a disgruntled

ex–Smith School student named Zachary Hazard tried to take over the world. We had to stop him. I'll admit we didn't follow our orders *exactly*, but the situation called for immediate action. Who knew that saving civilization as we know it was not a good enough excuse for breaking the rules?

"How could I forget?" Charlotte replies.

"But you don't care," Izumi says flatly.

"She cares a lot," I say.

Charlotte grins. "I do. So *much*. About who Mrs. Smith was talking about."

"We're going to spend the rest of our lives cleaning this campus," Izumi mutters.

We crawl back to the window and glance inside, making sure Mrs. Smith is gone. "Boost me up," I whisper. Izumi and Charlotte give me a shove over the window ledge. I fall headfirst into Mrs. Smith's office and freeze. What if she comes back? I can't very well say I'm pruning her desk fern. Quickly, I swipe the paper and throw myself back out the window. I have a lot of experience throwing myself from windows, so this is no big deal. The mound of decapitated rose heads cushions my landing. "Got it!"

We dash to the gazebo next to the Cavanaugh Family Meditative Pond and Fountain. It has shade, and if we sit in the corner we get a little bit of spray from the fountain.

Desperate times. Sweat drips from my forehead, making damp splotches on the paper.

"What does it say?" Charlotte asks, wedging in for a better view. I stink like mulch, and yet she manages to smell like rose petals. How does she do that? Izumi lies flat on the gazebo brick floor, blowing her straight dark bangs out of her eyes.

The girl on the paper is not me. Or any of us. That's bad. What makes it infinitely worse is whose name *is* on the paper.

Poppy Parsons.

Chapter 2

SMARTS. WITS. PRESSURE.

POPPY PARSONS *IS* EXCEPTIONAL, and she is the first one to say so. She speaks five languages, builds computers in her spare time, is nationally ranked in Fortnite, and runs the school's Dungeons and Dragons club (with an iron fist, apparently). She can run the mile in six minutes flat, is a black belt in karate, has an enviable cascade of honey-blond curls and a cute British accent, and once filed a complaint about me with the student disciplinary committee regarding the improper composting of an apple core. Needless to say, Poppy and I are *not* friends.

Izumi says Poppy has self-esteem issues, and that's why she talks constantly about her own awesomeness. She is really trying to convince *herself* that she is okay. This does not help me feel better about her name being on that paper rather than mine.

But I do feel pretty good about my new muscles, compliments of long hours of gardening, painting, scrubbing, and perfecting Deadhead the Rose. I have never been so strong in my life. When I see Toby on move-in day, I lift him clear off the ground to demonstrate. Toby is my other best friend, although different from Charlotte and Izumi.

"Put me down!" Toby howls, so I drop him like a sack of flour. He doesn't like that, either. "What is wrong with you?"

"I've spent a lot of time outdoors," I say, flexing an impressive bicep.

"Whatever." Suitcases and a big steamer trunk surround Toby. The lobby overflows with returning students and frazzled parents, all twirling in different directions. The headmaster's welcome-back lunch happens in an hour, but from the looks of this mess, everyone is going to be late.

"Abby!" Drexel Caine, Toby's dad and my biggest fan, hugs me so hard, I gasp.

"Drexel, let her go," Toby says with obvious disgust. Here at Smith we call our parents by their first names, just to annoy them. But Drexel seems downright tickled. He grins at Toby and tousles his hair like he's off to kinder-garten. "Son, I just love you guys. That's all."

Man, this is bad. Drexel has been lobotomized by hap-piness and second chances. Until last year, he was the poster parent for benign neglect. He forgot Toby's birth-day. He pulled a no-show on Parents' Weekend. He never made it to a single basketball game. He was too busy being the genius behind DrexCon to be bothered.

But when Zachary Hazard kidnapped him and he almost died, everything changed. Now he drinks his coffee from a WORLD'S #1 DAD! mug. Poor Toby. It's like a code-red emergency. Attentive parents can be a nightmare. Believe me, I *know*.

"Guess what?" Drexel rubs his hands together like a kid on Christmas morning about to dive into a mountain of presents. His eyes shine. "Tell her, Toby. Tell her!"

"Drexel," Toby hisses, but this does little. Drexel is per-manently thrilled by everything.

"Okay, I'll tell her," he says, practically jumping up and down. "DrexCon is sponsoring the Invitational Interschool Global Problems and Solutions Challenge this year. Isn't that the *best*?"

Wow, he really has gone off the deep end. The Invitational Interschool Global Problems and Solutions Challenge, or the

Challenge, as we call it, because its full name is just plain ridiculous, was started fifty years ago by Emma and Gemma Glass. As Jennifer likes to say, there's more than one way to save the world, and Emma and Gemma believed children should be encouraged to apply their classroom smarts to solving the many problems humans face, things like how to make sure everyone has enough food and clean water, a safe place to live, and an education. We come from so much privilege, the sisters said, don't we have an obligation to help those with less?

The Challenge was their answer, a biennial competition where teams of students perform three tasks around a theme: providing clean water, increasing the food supply, preventing wars, limiting pollution and creating clean energy, curing disease, recycling waste, and so on. The tasks test your smarts, your wits, and how well you perform under pressure. Smarts. Wits. Pressure.

To get invited, you have to have done something cool, like invent a garbage-eating robotic shark or figure out cheap travel to Mars or mastermind a peace process for the Middle East. Winners get full-on glory—international recognition and a pass to brag about being the best *forever*.

"Push kids out of their comfort zone," Emma said, "and they will surprise you." Or maybe it was Gemma? Anyway, I'm not surprised DrexCon is sponsoring this year's Challenge. Now that Drexel is in love with the world, he wants to make it better.

"That's exciting," I say, nudging Toby in the ribs. He ignores me.

"Smarts, wits, and pressure," Drexel says with a grin. "These kids that get invited are truly exceptional. I've missed so much!"

Back up a second. Did he say "exceptional"?

"And," Drexel continues, grinning, "I suggested Headmaster Smith send you four as a *team*. I have some influence as the lead sponsor." He winks conspiratorially. "I told the organizers all about that Cookie app you were working on this summer. How great am I?"

Toby goes pale. "Tell me you didn't. I don't *want* to do the Challenge."

"I did! And you do! I want the world to know how amazing you are! Of course, Mrs. Smith needs to approve, but I don't see that as a problem. Now why don't you two run along and get caught up? I'll get your stuff moved in, Tobes."

Tobes? This might be worse than I thought. As soon as we are out of earshot, Toby grabs my shoulders.

"I can't go on like this," he says, face tight with distress, curly black hair in a wild halo around his head. "He wants to hang out *all* the time. He makes me pancakes in animal shapes with chocolate chip eyeballs. He bought us *matching* baseball gloves."

"He calls you Tobes," I add.

"I'm losing my mind. You have no idea."

"Hey, remember my mother was headmaster last year. I know what it's like being under a microscope." We weave through a bunch of incoming Lower Middles, confused and scared, standing by parents who are also confused and scared. Nothing like boarding school drop-off day to make emotions run high.

"So where *is* Teflon, anyway?" Toby asks. Teflon is my mother's spy code name. I wish I were kidding.

"I don't know," I say. "Bulgaria? Romania? Beijing? The Himalayas? Back home in our apartment? If you're such a fan, why don't *you* keep track of her?"

Toby holds up his hands. "Okay. Got it. Don't ask about Teflon." We exit Main Hall and walk along the path toward McKinsey House dormitory, where I live.

"What's the Cookie app?" I ask.

"A failure, that's what," Toby snaps. "I can't believe Drexel told people about it! Basically, I spent all summer trying to figure out how to send a smell through a phone— you know, like attached to a text or something."

"Like stinky socks?" I ask.

"No! Like cookies or, I don't know, kittens."

"Kittens don't smell," I point out.

"You know what I mean," he growls. "Good things. Happy things. Jeez, what's wrong with wanting to spread a little happiness?"

"Nothing! What happened?"

"It didn't work," he grumbles. "I kept on practically poisoning myself. The cookie smell was toxic. I even barfed once."

"I'm sorry," I say. "I'm glad you're okay. Do you really think Drexel will get us invited to the Challenge?"

"Oh, I'm sure of it," Toby says with a grimace. "I mean, this is *Drexel Caine* we're talking about, even if version 2.0 is practically unrecognizable. For the record, we are *not* going to the Challenge. Everyone here already thinks I'm favored because of him."

And everyone is right. The new science and technology building is, after all, Caine Hall.

Dozens of girls buzz around McKinsey House in a state of move-in disarray. Izumi and Charlotte sit on a bench opposite the dorm and critically survey the chaos.

"You'd think after a hundred years," offers Charlotte, "they'd come up with a better way to move seven hundred and fifty-four students into their dorms at the same time."

"You'd think," concurs Izumi.

"Look who I found," I say.

"Welcome back, Toby," Charlotte says, grinning. "Where's Drexel?"

"Please, let's not talk about him."

"Oh, come on," says Izumi. "It's nice that your dad wants to spend time with you."

"All the time," I say. "*Every* day."

"Parents," Charlotte says with a shrug. "What are you going to do?"

While my mom is a superspy, Izumi's mom is the United States ambassador to Japan, and Charlotte's dad is richer than the entire country of Norway. At least none of them are boring. Toby plops down on the bench. Charlotte regales him with stories about our summer planting rosebushes and driving tractors around on the soccer field, but my mind is stuck on Drexel, the Challenge, and "exceptional."

"Did Abby tell you about Poppy?" Izumi asks. "The one who gets to be part of the spy school *before* she's sixteen?"

Toby narrows his gaze. "Poppy Parsons? In spy school? Like, *now*?" Before I came along and messed things up, Toby was Mrs. Smith's right-hand kid for spy gadgets. Now he has to wait until he's sixteen too.

"We overheard Mrs. Smith talking about it," Izumi clarifies. "Exceptions can be made for *exceptional* candidates. Like Veronica before and Poppy Parsons now."

Toby gets a moony look on his face whenever the name Veronica is mentioned. Veronica Brooks is a former Smith School superspy who begrudgingly trained me last year when Mrs. Smith wanted to use me as bait to find my missing mother. Veronica is also the object of Toby's unrequited affection.

We sit in silence for a minute, contemplating the great unfairness of Poppy Parsons. She has never once saved the world, at least not that we know of. She probably wouldn't even know where to start. What do we have to do to prove our worth?

And that's when it hits me. If being exceptional gets us into the spy school early, we have to prove our exceptionalness, and everyone knows the Challenge is where that is done. Challenge winners simply cannot be ignored. Sure, our chances of actually winning are slim, but can't we at least *try*? Now all I have to do is convince my friends that going is the most brilliant idea since electricity, since the Internet, since, I don't know, Fortnite!

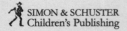